A Boy Called
BAT

A Boy Called BAT

WRITTEN BY
Elana K. Arnold

WITH PICTURES BY
Charles Santoso

WALDEN POND PRESS™
An Imprint of HarperCollins*Publishers*

HarperCollins
P U B L I S H E R S
Since 1817

Walden Pond Press is an imprint of HarperCollins Publishers.
Walden Pond Press and the skipping stone logo are trademarks and
registered trademarks of Walden Media, LLC.

A Boy Called Bat
Text copyright © 2017 by Elana K. Arnold
Illustrations copyright © 2017 by Charles Santoso
All rights reserved. Printed in the United States of America.
No part of this book may be used or reproduced in any manner
whatsoever without written permission except in the case of brief
quotations embodied in critical articles and reviews. For information
address HarperCollins Children's Books, a division of HarperCollins
Publishers, 195 Broadway, New York, NY 10007.
www.harpercollinschildrens.com

Library of Congress Control Number: 2016932066
ISBN 978-0-06-244582-7

Typography by Aurora Parlagreco
18 19 20 21   PC/LSCH   10 9 8 7 6
❖
First Edition

*For Max,
my wonderful boy*

Contents

CHAPTER 1
After School

Bixby Alexander Tam stared into the refrigerator, trying to decide what to eat. He knew that the longer he took, the more energy he was wasting, and Bixby Alexander Tam did not like to waste energy. But he also didn't like to eat leftovers, or cheese that had to be sliced, or any of the yogurt flavors in the fridge.

"Bat, close the refrigerator door!" yelled his

sister, Janie, from the kitchen table, where she sat cutting out pictures from a pile of old magazines. Janie, he was sure, had eaten all the lemon and vanilla yogurts. And she *knew* he only liked the creamy ones, not the fruit-on-the-bottom kind.

"Bat" was what almost everyone called Bixby Alexander Tam, for a couple of reasons: first, because the initials of his name—*B*, *A*, and *T*—spelled Bat.

But there were maybe other reasons. Bat's sensitive hearing, for one. He didn't like loud sounds. What was so unusual about that? And if Janie's old earmuffs happened to make an outstanding muffling device, was it that funny if he liked to wear them?

There was also the way he sometimes flapped his hands, when he was nervous or excited or thinking about something interesting. Some of the kids at school seemed to think that was *hilarious*.

And, of course, bats have wings, which they flap.

So, between the initials and the earmuffs and the hand flapping, the nickname had stuck.

And, truthfully, Bat didn't mind. Animals were his very favorite thing. Better even than vanilla yogurt.

"Janie, did you eat all the vanillas?"

"Not *all* of them," Janie answered. She curved the scissors around the bent arm of the boy she

was cutting out. "I saw you eat at least two or three of them."

"Did you eat the *last* vanilla?"

"Yes," said Janie, and with a final *snip*, she freed the shiny paper boy. "It was delicious."

Of course it was delicious. All the vanillas were delicious.

"Well," said Bat, closing the refrigerator door a little harder than he needed to, "now there is nothing to eat."

"I wouldn't say there's *nothing* to eat," teased Janie. She knew she wasn't supposed to tease him.

"Well, *I* would," said Bat. "Nothing I want to eat."

"Then you must not be very hungry."

On Tuesdays and Thursdays, after Mom drove Bat home from school, she had to go back to work for a couple more hours. It was Janie's job to watch Bat. Thursdays were the hardest, and today was a Thursday.

"Make me a snack," Bat demanded.

"Make me a snack, *what?*"

"Make me a snack *now.*"

"No," said Janie. "Make me a snack, *please.*"

"I don't have to say please," said Bat. "Making me an after-school snack is part of your job. You don't have to say please to get someone to do their job."

"You do if you want them to do it well," said Janie, but she pushed back the magazines and stood up.

Bat felt his elbows beginning to bend. He felt his hands getting ready to flap. "I'm *hungry,*" he said again. His voice sounded higher.

"Okay, okay," said Janie. "Don't fly away. I'll fix you peanut butter and jelly."

"Without the crusts," Bat said. He felt better already.

CHAPTER 2
Bat's Cave

After finishing his snack, Bat went to his room. Bat's room was his favorite place in the whole world. In his room, Bat felt completely comfortable. Here, he knew where everything was. If something was in the wrong place, it was his own fault, because no one messed with his room but him.

In the rest of their small house, Bat's mom and sister knew to put anything that needed to go to Bat's room in one of three baskets: his clean laundry basket, his book basket, and his miscellaneous stuff basket.

"Miscellaneous" was a great word, and one of Bat's favorites. It meant all the extra stuff, so the miscellaneous stuff basket could have almost anything (except clean laundry and books) in it.

When the baskets were full, Mom placed them in the hallway outside Bat's door. He took them into his room and unloaded them himself.

Once, Mom had tried to reorganize his dresser drawers because she thought he could "use some help." After, when he was so upset he couldn't even speak, she said, "I'm sorry, Bat, but your drawers were just a mess. Your hats mixed in with pants and sweaters. I don't know how you find *anything.*"

But the drawers weren't a mess. Not at all. If

Mom had looked more closely, she would have seen that his knit caps were in with his long pants and his sweaters, because he always wore those things together on cold days.

Shorts and T-shirts were in another drawer because he wore those things together on warm days.

"But what about *this* drawer?" Mom had asked, pulling open the bottom right drawer, which held a pair of pants, a wool sweater, and two T-shirts.

"Those are the things I never wear," Bat told her when he finally calmed down. "Because they're itchy and uncomfortable."

Then Mom cut the tags out of the T-shirts and Bat moved them to his warm-days drawer. After that, Mom "left him to his own devices," as she liked to say.

Once in his room, Bat closed the door. There

was a sign on the outside that said "Please Knock." Janie had written it for him, because her writing was much neater than his. Janie could do all the hand things better than Bat: write things, cut things out, smooth peanut butter on bread.

The clock told Bat that Mom would be home in forty-six minutes. Mom was a veterinarian, which was what Bat intended to be, too, one day. Mostly she treated cats and dogs, but sometimes she had "unusual patients." Once she had taken a BB pellet out of the wing of a hawk. The pellet had broken one of the bones and Mom had done surgery to mend it. She'd brought home X-rays to show Bat.

"Why would anyone shoot a hawk?" Bat had asked. "Do you think they were going to eat it?"

"No," said Mom. "Sometimes people do stupid things." She had been very angry about the hawk, angrier even than when Bat and Janie got into loud screaming fights. Seeing the X-ray of the hawk's broken wing made Bat angry, too.

But his room always made him feel better. It had a roll-down bamboo window shade and a fine closet full of shelves and a pull-out trundle in case someday a friend came to spend the night. It had a ceiling fan and a reading lamp and a rug with a picture of a train track printed on it.

Bat felt like looking through his animal encyclopedia, which he often did after school, so he

pulled it down from the bookshelf and dropped comfortably onto his beanbag. His stomach was full of sandwich and Mr. Grayson hadn't assigned any homework. For this moment, at least, Bat felt perfectly content.

CHAPTER 3
No Vanilla Yogurt

Mom was supposed to be home by five o'clock. But five o'clock came, and Mom did not arrive. By five fifteen, Bat wanted to call the police.

"That's what we're supposed to do in case of emergency," he said to Janie. She was watching TV.

"This isn't an emergency, Bat."

"How do you know? It might be an emergency. You don't know for sure that it isn't an emergency."

"Bat, call Mom's phone if you're so worried."

Bat didn't want to call Mom's phone. What if she was driving, and she answered when he called, and then she crashed the car?

"I don't want to cause an emergency," he said.

"If you had any friends to play with," Janie said, "you could hang out with them on Tuesdays and Thursdays instead of being a pain in my neck."

Bat thought this was unfair, and also mean, considering that he was so worried, but before he could say anything, he heard Mom's car turn in to the driveway. A warm rush of relief flooded over him. He left Janie in front of the TV and ran outside. "Mom," he said. "You're late."

"Easy, Bat," Mom said, climbing out of the car. "No need to be angry."

Bat wasn't angry. Not really. He was relieved. But instead of explaining this, Bat asked, "Did you go to the grocery store and get more vanilla yogurt?"

"I didn't have time," Mom said.

That was the last straw. Mom was late and Bat was worried and now NO VANILLA YOGURT.

Bat felt a ball of anger rising up in his chest, hot and hard and loud, wanting to escape through his mouth in a yell. His eyes squinted together and his hands drew up tight against the sides of his body.

Mom put her hand on his shoulder and knelt down so she could look right into Bat's eyes. But Bat didn't want to look at her eyes. He didn't want her eyes looking at him.

"Calm down, Bat," Mom said in her soothing voice, the one she saved for when Bat was getting really upset. "It's okay. I had a good reason for not going to the grocery store. If you can calm yourself down, I can tell you what it is."

Bat didn't care what Mom's reason was. She should have gone to the store. She knew how much he liked vanilla yogurt, and it was her job to buy it for him. Bat didn't have any money or a

car. If Mom didn't buy him yogurt, there would be no yogurt.

But then Mom said, "It was because of an animal. A baby animal."

CHAPTER 4
Is It a . . .

"What kind of animal?" asked Bat.

"You'll see," Mom answered. She walked around to the back of the station wagon and opened the door.

"Is it a puppy?" asked Bat.

"You'll see," Mom answered, taking out a cardboard box with air holes poked into the top.

"Is it a kitten?" Bat asked as he followed her to the front door.

"You'll see," Mom answered.

"Is it a duckling?" Bat asked as he bounced up and down, hands flapping excitedly.

"You'll see," Mom answered. "Open the door for me, okay?"

Bat pushed open the front door. "Is it a hoglet?"

Mom laughed. "Where would I get a baby hedgehog?"

"I don't know," Bat said. Then he had an awful thought. "Is it a baby human?"

Mom walked into the living room. Janie, still watching the TV, called out, "Hey. You're late."

"I know," Mom said to Janie. And then she said to Bat, "Bat, honey, I wouldn't put a baby human in a cardboard box. And anyway, would a baby human be so bad?"

"Yes," said Bat firmly.

"Well, it's not a baby human," said Mom.

Now Janie was interested. She got up to have a closer look. "What's in the box?" she asked.

"Mom brought home a baby animal," Bat yelled in a rush, trying to be the one to tell Janie, and that way she'd know that he had known about it first.

"Jeez, Bat, don't scream in my face! Twelve inches, remember?"

Bat was supposed to stay at least twelve inches away from Janie when he talked to her. She didn't like it when he got too close. There were lots of rules when it came to Janie.

"How did you do on that math test?" Mom asked Janie. "Did the chart we made help?"

Bat bounced up and down on the balls of his feet, pulling the collar of his shirt into his mouth and sucking on the fabric. They were going to talk about a math test? *Now?*

"Mo-o-m," he groaned.

"Okay, okay," she said. "We can talk about math later. Come on. Let's go into the kitchen. There is someone I want you to meet."

CHAPTER 5
A Tiny Pink Nose

Mom set the box on the kitchen table.

"Is it sleeping?" Bat asked, his voice a whisper.

"Probably," Mom said. "Babies sleep most of the time."

"What is it?" Janie asked.

"Bat, do you want to open the lid?"

Bat didn't answer. He was too excited. Very carefully, he lifted the lid of the box and peered inside. Janie stood behind him, breathing on his ear.

"You're breathing on my ear," Bat said.

Janie ignored him. "It's just a bunch of rags," she said.

Mom walked around to the far side of the round table and reached into the box. She scooped up the pile of material and sat down. "Look."

Bat watched as Mom shifted the towel in her arms. A nose peeked out—a tiny pink nose—and then two slanted-closed eyes, a forehead covered in downy fuzz, little ears still curled tight against its head.

Janie began, "Is that a—"

"It's a kit," Bat said, enchanted by the tiny creature, wanting so badly to hold it. "A baby skunk."

"Oh, Mom," Janie said. "I can't believe you brought home a skunk!"

"I had to," Mom said, rubbing the skunk's little forehead with her thumb. "He's an orphan."

"O-oh," breathed Janie. She leaned in closer, blocking Bat's view. "How old is he?"

"You're in my way," Bat said loudly, and he pushed Janie's arm to make room for himself.

"Bat," Mom said, "you need to stay calm around the skunk kit. Okay? You don't want to scare him."

Bat did not want to scare the skunk kit. He wanted to hold the skunk kit, maybe even feed and care for the skunk kit. But his sister was standing in his way.

"Move, Janie," he hissed at her, as quietly as he could hiss.

"Why don't you both sit down," Mom said. "I'll tell you all about him."

Janie plopped down into the chair on Mom's right, so Bat went around to her other side and sat in the chair on her left. He scooted the chair as close to Mom's as he could. The kit was still tucked into the towel, only his little face visible. Eyes closed, he opened his mouth in a yawn, his tiny pink tongue arching out.

Mom said, "Bat, do you remember when we smelled that skunk on the way to school this morning?"

Bat did remember. They had smelled it just after they'd pulled off their street, Plum Lane, and onto Anderson Road.

He had smelled it, and Mom had smelled it, too. Bat had craned his neck, looking out each window carefully. He'd seen lots of people on bicycles—they lived near a college and the students mostly rode bikes to class—and he'd seen other cars, and some people on foot. It was the beginning of spring, but it was still cold, so he had seen lots of hats and scarves.

He'd seen an American flag on a flagpole in front of the post office. He'd seen a red bus. He'd seen a sign that read "Welcome to Quincy, a

Bike-Friendly Town." But he had not seen a skunk.

Bat nodded. "I remember," he said.

"Well, unfortunately, the skunk we smelled but didn't see was the mama skunk. A car hit her, and a couple of college students brought her to my office in the basket of a bike. She was there waiting for me after I dropped you off at school, injured and very pregnant."

"Is she okay?" Janie asked.

"I wish I could say she is," Mom answered. "I wasn't able to save the mother, or the other baby kits. Only this one lived. I was able to check the mother for diseases, though, and luckily she wasn't sick, which is a good sign the kit isn't sick, either."

"That's awesome," Bat said.

"Bat!" said Janie, loud and sharp. The kit twitched and shifted, scared by Janie's voice.

"How can you say it's awesome? The mom died! The other babies died!"

Bat didn't mean that it was awesome that the other skunks had died. Of course that wasn't awesome. He'd meant that it was awesome that *this* kit had lived.

But it wasn't worth it to try to explain to Janie what he'd meant. She usually misunderstood Bat. Most everyone did.

"Can I?" Bat reached out for the kit, wanting so badly to hold him that his fingers twitched.

"We can't keep him," Mom warned. "There's a wild animal rescue center that we can give him to in about a month, but they're too busy to take him just yet. So we can help him get bigger and stronger before we hand him over to the experts. They'll raise him until he's ready to be released into the wild, when he's about five months old."

Then she passed the tiny kit, wrapped in towels, into Bat's arms.

The kit was so small that Bat couldn't even tell he was in the towel except for the tiny face that peeked out. He cradled the bundle in his arms. He felt his face stretch into a wide smile, so wide it made his cheeks sore.

CHAPTER 6
Skunk Lunch

"Can it spray yet?" Janie asked.

"No," Mom answered. "Soon he will be able to. But when skunks are babies, they can't spray as strongly as the adults."

Bat realized that he didn't know a lot about skunks. He knew they sprayed a stinky smell to protect themselves, and he knew they were mammals, and he knew they were omnivores because they ate bugs and smaller animals and plants, too.

But he didn't know very much more than that. He decided to learn everything about skunks.

"What are we going to feed him?" Bat asked. "Can I do it?"

"He's too little to eat yet, so we need to feed him formula. They don't make skunk formula, so we use puppy formula. It's the closest thing to mother-skunk milk."

Janie stood up. "It's a cute skunk, Mom, but I want to go over to Ezra's house. Okay?"

"Okay," Mom said. "Be back in an hour."

Ezra lived three houses up the block and had been Janie's best friend since before Bat was born. Janie loved Ezra. She thought he was funny and smart and creative. Bat didn't love Ezra. He thought Ezra was loud and annoying and a mean tease.

Sometimes, when Janie went to play at Ezra's house, it bothered Bat that he wasn't invited, and that there wasn't a house he was invited to visit where Janie didn't go. But right now he didn't care about Ezra, or about anything other than feeding the skunk kit. "Good-bye," he said to Janie without taking his eyes off the baby skunk's tiny face. The skunk was yawning and licking his lips with the world's tiniest, pinkest tongue.

Janie left. Mom said, "Okay, Bat, sit right here and I'll get the formula."

She went to her bag and pulled out a can, like a soda can but with a picture of a puppy on it. Mom shook it and cracked it open and dipped a syringe inside, pulling the plunger up. Bat watched it fill with a thick white liquid.

"We only give him a few drops at a time," Mom said, carrying the full syringe back over to the table. "Watch me do it first."

She took the skunk and arranged him on her lap, one hand over his back and under his front legs to hold him upright, the other hand aiming the syringe full of formula at his mouth. The skunk seemed to know what was about to happen and twitched his little pink nose back and forth eagerly.

Mom slowly pushed down on the plunger, and Bat watched a thick white droplet of puppy formula push through the hole at the end of the syringe. The skunk tipped back his chin and opened his mouth, licking eagerly at it.

"What a good little baby," Mom crooned, pressing more formula into his mouth.

"I want to feed him. Let me feed him. I want to feed him," Bat said.

"Okay, okay." Mom handed the skunk back to

Bat. He tried to hold the skunk the way Mom had, and then took the syringe in his other hand.

"Very slowly," Mom warned him.

And finally it was Bat's turn. As slowly as he could, he pressed down on the plunger, aiming the syringe tip at the baby skunk's mouth. And it worked!

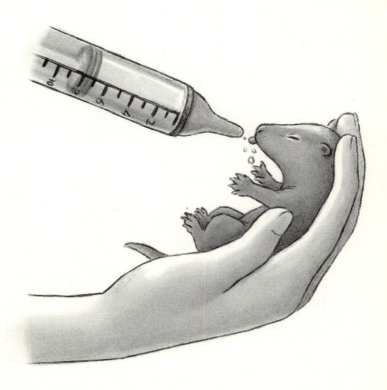

The skunk's little pink tongue lapped at the formula. Droplets gathered at the corners of his mouth, and some ran down his chin onto the towel, but most of it made it into the baby skunk.

"I'm doing it," Bat whispered. "I'm feeding him."

"You sure are," Mom said.

Bat knew he was doing a messier job of it than Mom had done, but the baby skunk didn't seem to mind.

"I love him," Bat said. He hadn't meant to say it out loud.

Mom laughed. "Careful, or you might make me jealous," she said.

"But it's true," Bat said. "I love him."

Mom said they'd have to hand the kit over to the rescue center in a month. But Bat, holding the tiny animal in his arms, made a silent promise that he'd figure out a way to keep him.

CHAPTER 7

Every-Other Fridays

The next morning was an Every-Other Friday. On Every-Other Fridays, Mom drove Bat to his school, and Janie walked to her school just like usual, but in the afternoon, Dad would pick them up—first Bat, whose class let out twenty minutes before Janie's—and they would all go home to his apartment for the weekend.

Every-Other Fridays made Bat uncomfortable,

like his skin was on too tight. Bat liked it when things followed a pattern, and Every-Other Fridays broke the pattern. This Every-Other Friday was the worst one Bat had ever experienced, because it meant that it would be *three days* until he saw the skunk kit again.

He had begged Mom to let him take the skunk to Dad's house. But Mom refused. "The baby skunk needs to be with me," she said. "I'll take him to work and the vet techs can watch him while I'm with patients. Besides, Bat, I don't think your dad is a fan of skunks."

Bat even tried pretending to be sick so that he could stay home instead of going to school. He told Mom that he had a sore throat and achy ears. Bat hardly *ever* lied. It made him feel itchy. But even though Mom's patients were animals rather than humans, she was still a kind of doctor. She shined a light into his ears and made him say *ahh* as she looked down his throat.

"You're not sick, Bat," she said. "You just want to stay with the skunk kit."

"He *needs* me," Bat whined.

"Bat," Mom warned, "don't let yourself get all worked up, okay?"

"Sorry, sorry," said Bat.

"We can help raise the kit this month as a family, as long as you keep on doing all the regular stuff, too. School and Dad's and homework and everything. If the skunk kit is too big of a distraction, then I can get Laurence to take him home in the evenings."

Laurence was Bat's favorite vet tech at Mom's clinic. He could juggle five juggling clubs, and even though he had enormous hands, big enough to hold all five clubs at once, he was gentle. He had the deepest voice Bat had ever heard, deep like space.

But no matter how much Bat liked Laurence, there was no way he was going to let him take the kit home after work.

"My throat feels better," he said. "Much better."

Mom and Janie and Bat all left the house together. Mom locked the door behind them. She kissed Janie and said, "Look both ways. Have a fun weekend."

"Okay, Mom," Janie said. "See you on Monday."

Bat climbed into the backseat of the car and fastened his seat belt. He liked to sit in the middle seat because someone had once told him that it was the safest seat in the whole car. That was one of the things he didn't like about Every-Other Fridays. His dad's car, a fast little yellow convertible, didn't have a middle backseat. It just had two side backseats, with a hump in between.

Mom placed the box with the skunk kit on the front passenger seat. Then she started the car and backed down the driveway. It wasn't a long drive to Bat's school. The distance from their house to his school was exactly 2.3 miles. Bat knew this because he liked his mother to push the button on the dashboard each morning, the one that reset the trip meter.

Bat spent the entire 2.3 miles trying to come up with a reason why he shouldn't go to Dad's even though it was an Every-Other Friday, a reason that wouldn't make his mom give the kit to Laurence. But he couldn't think of anything.

They arrived at his school. "You'll take care of the kit?" Bat asked Mom.

"Honey," Mom said. "I'm a veterinarian. Taking care of animals is my job. I promise."

Bat nodded. He unbuckled his seat belt, slid across the backseat, and got out of the car.

"Wait a minute," Mom called after him through her rolled-down window. "Aren't you forgetting something?"

He had his backpack. He had his lunch. He had his earmuffs. "No," he said.

Mom smiled. "You forgot to kiss me good-bye."

"Oh yeah," said Bat. He walked back over to the

car and stuck his head through Mom's window.

She wrapped her arms around his neck and pulled him close. Her wavy brown hair tickled his nose. "Good-bye, little Bat," she said. "I'll miss you." Then she kissed his cheek.

"Good-bye," Bat answered. He walked up to the school's front door, then turned around. Mom was still there, in her car, watching him. He raised his hand and waved. Mom honked the horn at him— three light, happy honks—and then she drove away.

CHAPTER 8
Sixteen Eyelets

///

Sometimes Bat wished that Janie went to his school, because it would be kind of neat to see her in the hallways and at lunchtime, but most of the time he was glad that his school was something he didn't have to share with her. Janie attended the Robert E. Willett Elementary School, but this was her last year. Next fall she would be going to junior high school.

Bat went to a private school. It had smaller classes than the public school, and his parents thought it was a "better fit for him," which was fine with Bat. Mr. Grayson was a good teacher who never yelled and who usually let Bat wear his ear-muffs if things got too loud. Also, his school—the Saw Whet School—was named after a type of owl.

The main hallway of the Saw Whet School was a busy place until 8:35 a.m., when class officially started. Until then, it was full of parents walking the younger kids (those in kindergarten and first grade) to their classrooms and older kids walking themselves, all while the principal, Mrs. Martinez, stood outside of the administration office, smiling and being friendly.

"Bat!" called Mrs. Martinez, waving and smiling.

Bat didn't feel like talking to Mrs. Martinez, so he pretended he didn't see her and slid to the far

side of the hallway as he passed. That way she couldn't reach out and rumple his hair.

Bat hated it when people rumpled his hair, and Mrs. Martinez loved to rumple hair. She had never yet rumpled *his* hair, and Bat wanted to keep it that way.

Bat liked the main hallway better when all the other kids were in their classrooms. Right now, Lucca and Israel, two kids in Bat's same class, were struggling out of their rain boots on the big rubber mat. It wasn't raining, but dark clouds peppered the sky in a way that could mean that recess would be wet. At Saw Whet School, one of the philosophies was that students should go outside rain or shine or snow.

Bat hadn't worn rain boots, so he didn't have any that he needed to take off. He didn't carry an umbrella, either, because the Saw Whet School didn't allow them in the hallways or classrooms, which Bat agreed was a wise decision. He skirted around a kindergartner whose mother was kneeling in front of him, holding a tissue to his nose—"Blow," she said—and he dodged between a couple of big kids, sixth graders who were tossing a small red rubber ball back and forth.

"Balls are supposed to be kept outside," Bat told the slightly smaller of the two big kids, a boy he recognized by the red glasses he wore.

"Not this ball," said the boy. "This is a special ball." Then he threw the ball over Bat's head, to the other kid, a very tall girl who caught it expertly with one hand and laughed.

"It looks like a regular ball," Bat said.

"It's not a regular ball," said the boy with red glasses.

Bat had a weird feeling in his stomach, like the boy was tricking him. He didn't know what to say.

Just then Lucca and Israel came by, without their rain boots. "Hi, Bat," Israel said. "Do you think it'll rain?"

"Maybe," said Bat. "Well, eventually, yes, but today, maybe."

Relieved, Bat watched the two big kids move away toward their classroom, still tossing the ball. "What do you think was special about that ball?" he asked Israel.

"Nothing," Israel said.

Then Miss Kiko came out of the kindergarten room and rang her handbell. It made a gentle tinkling sound, way better than the harsh, painful scream of Janie's electric school-bell system, which Bat had heard last year during a school play he'd gone to watch.

"To class, to class, it's time for another day!" Miss Kiko had a beautiful voice, which was probably why it was her job to announce the start of school.

Bat followed Lucca and Israel into Mr. Grayson's third-grade classroom.

"I brought two sandwiches for lunch today," Lucca was telling Israel, "in case you want to trade cookies for one."

"Why would I want to do that?" Israel answered. "I brought my own sandwich."

Bat knew why Lucca would think Israel wanted to trade. Yesterday he had heard Lucca tell Israel that she didn't really like her cream cheese sandwiches, and Israel had replied that he didn't like the turkey one his mom always made. "I would trade anything for a cream cheese sandwich," he had said.

He listened to see if Lucca would remind Israel

of what he had said, but she didn't.

"Probably Israel was just being nice," Bat interjected, "to make you feel better about bringing cream cheese sandwiches to school every day. He probably didn't really want your sandwich."

Israel turned around. His face was red and his eyebrows pointed toward each other, making a wrinkly crinkle in his forehead. "Dude," he said to Bat.

Bat waited for Israel to say more, but he didn't. Just that one word—"Dude."

Then Lucca started crying, and she shoved past Bat to go back into the hallway. He watched her run into the girls' bathroom.

Mr. Grayson came over. He was wearing his bright-orange tennis shoes today. Bat liked it when he wore those shoes. It was like he was wearing suns on his feet.

"What's the problem, friends?" he asked.

"Bat embarrassed Lucca," Israel said, really loudly, making Bat wish he had his earmuffs. They were in his backpack, on his back.

"I'm sure you didn't mean to embarrass her, did you, Bat?" asked Mr. Grayson. There were sixteen eyelets on each of his shoes, Bat counted. Eight

on the left side, eight on the right side. That made thirty-two eyelets.

"Bat, can you look up at my face?" Mr. Grayson asked.

Bat shook his head. Thirty-two eyelets. His own shoes had half as many. Sixteen eyelets, four on each side of each shoe.

Mr. Grayson sighed. "Okay, Bat, go sit at your table."

Bat wondered if anyone in the class had more eyelets in their shoes than Mr. Grayson. He kept his eyes on shoes as he walked through the classroom. Nope. No one did.

CHAPTER 9
Open-Door
Babycakes Policy

Mr. Grayson was a good teacher for lots of reasons: he let kids eat snacks at their desk if they were hungry. He didn't make students ask permission to go to the bathroom. He didn't believe in making people apologize. ("You can't *make* someone be sorry," he always said.)

And he believed in class pets. That's how he put it. "I believe in class pets," he had said on the first

day of class when he introduced them to Babycakes, the class rabbit. Babycakes, a white angora
bunny that looked like a giant fluff ball, lived in a
pen in the back of the room, near the bookshelves.
It was a big pen, with a gate.

"If anyone ever needs to cuddle," Mr. Grayson
said, "Babycakes is there for you."

And that was the thing that made Mr. Grayson
the best teacher Bat had ever had: his "open-door
Babycakes policy," which meant that any time
a kid needed to cuddle, he or she could go visit
Babycakes, no permission needed, no questions
asked.

Babycakes liked carrots and apples and put up
with the cuddling. Bat knew the rabbit liked treats
better than kids, but he also knew that Babycakes
was smart enough to realize that the two often
went together.

The thing about Mr. Grayson's open-door Babycakes policy was that none of the kids wanted to
ruin it by overusing it. Bat was Babycakes's most
frequent visitor; Israel visited the second most
often, and then probably Jenny was third. A couple of months ago, Israel had given Bat a drawing
he'd done of Babycakes. It was pretty good. Bat
usually tried to visit Babycakes during recess or

lunch, when a visit wouldn't mean leaving group time. But today he didn't think he could wait until recess. Maybe because he missed the baby skunk so much.

When Mr. Grayson had everyone pull out the money game, Payday, that they played on Fridays, Bat slipped away from his table and headed to the back of the room. Today, Babycakes wasn't sleeping. She was just sitting in her favorite spot, on top of the plastic hutch where she slept. She looked like white cotton candy.

Bat sat close to Babycakes and put his hand on her back, just to let her know he was there. He didn't want to startle her.

"Break into groups of four," Mr. Grayson said. "Choose a banker and pay everyone two hundred dollars."

For a moment, Bat thought maybe Mr. Grayson

was going to let him skip the game and just hang out with Babycakes. But then he said, "Bat, five minutes."

Bat didn't want to play Payday. He didn't want to join the class in five minutes. But the open-door Babycakes policy didn't mean it was okay to skip stuff that the class was doing. It was one of those unspoken rules that Mom was always talking about—those things that people are supposed to know without having to be told.

Bat hated unspoken rules, but he loved the open-door Babycakes policy, so when five minutes later Mr. Grayson said, "Okay, Bat, time's up," Bat reluctantly scooted Babycakes off his lap where he had set her and rejoined the class.

The games were all arranged. Jenny Pearson had dealt out two hundred dollars for Bat. Lucca, Bat saw, had returned from the bathroom with red-rimmed eyes. She was in a different group.

"Ready?" Jenny asked.

"I guess," said Bat, and he sat in the empty seat between Jenny and Raymond. Across from him, Cory rolled the dice. Bat sighed. It was going to be a long day.

CHAPTER 10
A Very Long Day

Bat was right. It *was* a long day. The rain that had been threatening came, and after they ate lunch, the students pulled on rain gear to splash in puddles. Bat did not like to get wet. He didn't like it *at all*. It made his clothes feel sticky and itchy and uncomfortable.

Mr. Grayson knew that Bat didn't like to get wet, so even though the Saw Whet school philosophy said that students should go outside rain or shine or snow, he asked Bat, "Would you like to spend recess helping me clean Babycakes's enclosure?"

"Yes," said Bat.

Mr. Grayson got a trash bag and Bat scooped the old straw into it. Then they laid out a fresh batch of straw. It smelled like summertime and sunshine.

Babycakes hopped over to the straw and sniffed it.

"She looks happy," Mr. Grayson said.

"She looks exactly the same as she always does," Bat answered.

Mr. Grayson laughed. Grown-ups were always laughing at things that Bat didn't think were funny, but it didn't bother Bat very much when Mr. Grayson did it.

Julio, a fourth grader who everyone said was

"a natural athlete," came into the classroom. "Mr. Grayson," he said, "Principal Martinez wants to know if you're still going to teach yoga."

"Sure, sure," Mr. Grayson said. "Tell her I'm all ready to start." Then he said, "Julio, I think you've grown a foot since the last time I saw you."

Julio shrugged. "Not that much," he said, "but I've grown an inch since winter break."

"I'm not surprised," Mr. Grayson said. "That was three months ago."

Bat thought about time as he followed Mr. Grayson to the yoga room and as he sat on his mat in the butterfly pose. Three months, he guessed, could be a little bit of time or a really long time, depending on who you were.

For instance, a monarch butterfly born in the summer lives only about six weeks, so four months would feel like forever, but a monarch butterfly born in the winter might live for eight months, so four months would be just half its life.

And if you were a boy with a skunk kit that you were only allowed to keep for one month, time was sure to pass much, much too quickly.

Bat considered telling Mr. Grayson about the life cycle of the monarch butterfly, but the teacher was busy unlacing his orange high-tops and getting ready to lead the group in yoga. He decided he would talk about monarch butterflies with Mr. Grayson later.

But the right "later" never happened. After yoga they went back to the third-grade room for reading circle. After reading circle they worked on their volcano projects, which Bat had not been looking forward to.

Groups of four kids had to work together to build a volcano. Mr. Grayson called it "collaborative art." Bat did not like collaboration. He liked to do things himself. That way, if something didn't turn out the way he wanted it to, there was no one else to be mad at, and if he wanted to take it apart and start over, no one could tell him not to.

But Mr. Grayson wouldn't let Bat be a group of one.

The problem was that no one else in the group seemed to care as much as Bat did. Three times before two forty-five, when class was finally over for the day, Bat's group said, "Mr. Grayson, Bat won't let us help!"

"I don't need help," Bat told Jenny when she complained for a second time.

"It's a *group* project," she said. "You *have* to let us help."

Israel, who was in Bat's group, kept asking him all kinds of annoying questions, like, "Hey, Bat, do you think the lava is red enough?" and "Bat, can you pass me the paste?"

Bat ignored the lava question, but about the paste he said, "Glue works better than paste. The paste gets all weird and flaky when it dries."

"Okay," said Israel. "Pass me then glue, then."

"I'm using the glue," Bat said.

Things would go much more smoothly, Bat thought, if the other kids would stop asking questions and interfering, and just let him get on with the job.

By the time Miss Kiko rang the end-of-day bell from the hallway, Bat's left eye felt twitchy. All he wanted to do was climb into Mom's car and go home to his own room.

But when he walked outside, he didn't see Mom's burgundy station wagon. Instead he saw Dad's yellow sports car, and he remembered with a heavy sigh that today was an Every-Other Friday, and he wouldn't get to see his own room—or the baby kit—for three long days.

If Bat were a mayfly, he wouldn't even live that long.

CHAPTER 11
Apartment 2A

"Hi, sport!" said Dad.

Bat didn't like being called "sport" because he didn't like playing sports or watching sports. Bat liked being called Bat, because he liked playing with animals and reading about animals and watching videos about animals.

But Dad didn't like calling him Bat. When he wasn't calling Bat "sport," he always called him

Bixby Alexander.

"It's a great name," he liked to say.

It was an okay name. Bat's first name, Bixby, had been his mom's last name before she got married. Now that she and Dad were divorced, she could have made it her last name again, but she kept Tam, instead, because, as she said, "I gave Bixby to you, and you get to keep it."

Bat's middle name, Alexander, was the same as his dad's middle name. And all four of them—Dad, Mom, Janie, and Bat—were Tams, even though they didn't all live together in one house.

The rain had turned into a gentle mist, and Dad had his windshield wipers turned on to their lowest setting.

"You know what we need on a chilly day like this?" Dad asked.

"What?" Bat replied.

"Well, I was thinking that, after we pick up your

sister, we could all go to Cocoa's to get some hot chocolate. Do you like that idea?"

Cocoa's was the name of Bat's favorite coffee shop, downtown. It was nestled in between a bookstore that also sold stuffed animals and a shoe store.

"Okay," said Bat. They drove under a little bridge and through downtown. Because of the rain, fewer bicyclists crowded the streets, and it didn't take Bat's dad very long to get to Janie's school.

Bat recognized her right away. She was standing near the corner, wearing her bright-yellow rain slicker. Bat admired the way she looked, like a shiny yellow sun.

"Hi, Dad," said Janie. She tossed her backpack into the seat next to Bat and then slid into the front seat, slamming the door.

"Hello, my girl. How was your day?"

Bat relaxed in the backseat as Janie told Dad about her day. He didn't listen to the words of what she was saying, but he liked the way her voice went up and down like music. Dad's voice was nice, too. It was lower than Janie's and it didn't go up and down very much. It was like a straight line.

At Cocoa's, Bat spilled some of his hot chocolate on his shirt when he took off the lid to add cinnamon.

"Be careful, sport," said Dad, which was a dumb thing to say because the hot chocolate was already spilled and being careful now wouldn't unspill it. Bat couldn't enjoy the taste of his drink at all

because the only thing he could think about was the wet, uncomfortable stain on his shirt.

Dad's apartment was in a complex that had a pool and a workout room. Kids under thirteen weren't allowed to use the workout equipment, which Bat thought was unfair. He really wanted to try the treadmill.

The apartment was on the second floor. There was an elevator, but Bat preferred to take the stairs. He liked them because there were two sets of eleven stairs, and eleven was his favorite number. One day he would be eleven, which felt like an exciting thing to be.

At the top of the stairs, they turned right and walked around the corner. Then Dad unlocked the door of apartment 2A and they all went inside.

"Home sweet home," said Dad.

It didn't feel like home, and it didn't smell sweet.

"It smells like onions in here," Janie said, wrinkling her nose.

"That's because the slow cooker made dinner for us," Dad said. "Chili."

Bat didn't like chili. Dad knew he didn't like it.

Bat didn't like mushy foods, except for oatmeal with brown sugar.

"I don't like chili," Bat said.

"Maybe you'll like it tonight," Dad answered. "I tried a new recipe."

Unless the new recipe was for a chili that didn't include any chili, Bat would not like it.

Bat sighed and shrugged off his backpack. It was going to be a long weekend.

CHAPTER 12
Finally

On Monday afternoon, after Miss Kiko rang the bell, Bat walked outside as fast as he could without running. Running was not allowed in the school hallway. Bat couldn't wait to go home to his very own room. He couldn't wait to see the baby kit again.

He had called Mom every day to ask about the kit, and she had called him each night to tell him a story before he went to sleep. But now, finally, he would get to see the kit and smell its fur and feed it with a dropper. And maybe Mom would even let him name the kit. He had thought all weekend about a good name and he thought he finally had the perfect one. He couldn't wait to tell Mom.

But Mom's burgundy station wagon wasn't in the line of waiting cars. Israel's mom was there, in her tall blue van, and Jenny Pearson's grandmother was there, in her little green bug. One by one Bat watched his classmates climb into cars—blue cars, white cars, black cars, clean cars, and dirty cars.

No Mom car.

Suddenly Bat felt a hand on his shoulder. It was a man's hand, with three silver rings. Mr. Grayson's hand.

"Your mom must be running late, huh, Bat?"

asked Mr. Grayson. Up close like this, Bat noticed a line of hard, short little hairs just sprouting above his teacher's upper lip. Was Mr. Grayson trying to grow a mustache?

"Mr. Grayson," Bat said, "did you know that gorillas can catch human colds and other illnesses?"

"Is that so," said Mr. Grayson.

"It is," said Bat. Sometimes, when Bat was nervous about something—like right now, when he was nervous about where his mother was and why she was late—he thought about interesting animal facts.

"Well, did *you* know," said Mr. Grayson, "that if you lift a kangaroo's tail off the ground, it can't hop?"

"Yes," said Bat. "Doesn't everyone know that?"

Mr. Grayson laughed. The stubby little hairs above his lip bobbed up and down. "Maybe so," he said.

Bat considered whether he should tell Mr. Grayson that his mustache looked a lot like a caterpillar. But just then Mom pulled up in her burgundy wagon. She waved and honked her normal three friendly honks.

"There she is," said Mr. Grayson.

"I know," said Bat. "I can see her."

Mr. Grayson sighed and rubbed his finger along his upper lip. "Okay, Bat," he said. "Have a good afternoon." He waved at Bat's mom before walking away, across the parking lot to his own car. It was a little orange coupe, usually dusty, but clean today because of the rain over the weekend.

Bat opened the back door of the station wagon and climbed in, slipping out of his backpack before he shut the door.

"Hello, Bat!" said Mom.

"Hello," said Bat. He buckled his seat belt. "You're late."

"I know," Mom said. "I'm sorry." She turned around from the front seat to smile at him. "I missed you," she said. Then she turned back around and started driving toward home.

"I missed you, too," Bat said. "Dad made chili and wouldn't let me watch the animal channel because there was a basketball game and Janie was busy all weekend practicing that song for her stupid play."

Janie loved to sing and dance and act, and she was getting ready to audition for the role of Alice in *Alice in Wonderland*, her school's spring play.

"Is she getting good at the audition song?" Mom asked.

"I don't know," Bat said. "How is the baby kit? Is he at home?"

"Yes," said Mom. "I set up an enclosure for him in the living room."

"Like Babycakes's enclosure?"

"Not that big," Mom said.

As they turned the corner onto their street, Plum Lane, Bat saw Janie up ahead on the sidewalk. He could tell it was her by the way her dark-brown ponytail swung side to side. Her hair was thick and straight like a horse's tail, which was why Bat liked it, even though he would never tell Janie.

CHAPTER 13
What's in a Name

The enclosure was nothing like Babycakes's enclosure. It was just a dog kennel, a smallish one, blue plastic with a handle on the top and a black grate door that locked. But inside Mom had made a nice nest out of old ripped-up T-shirts.

"Did you use any of mine?" Bat asked.

"I did," Mom said. "I hope that's okay."

"It's better than okay," Bat answered. "If the

T-shirts still have my scent, then maybe the kit will bond with me."

"I don't think we could get your scent out of your T-shirts if we tried, Bat," said Janie.

"That's teasing," said Bat, but he was peering into the enclosure and didn't feel very upset.

"Did you use any of mine, Mom?" Janie asked.

"No," Mom said. "Don't worry."

"I don't see him," Bat said. "I don't see him anywhere."

"He's definitely in there, Bat," Mom said. "The door was latched and everything. And he's still too little to walk, anyway. His eyes aren't even open yet."

Bat unlatched the door and stuck his hand inside. Yes. There was the kit. Tiny and warm, wrapped in a fold of fabric.

"He's safe," Bat said.

"Okay, Bat," Mom said, "latch up the cage and go wash your hands. Let's have a snack."

At the table, Janie was smearing peanut butter on crackers. She'd gotten out a second butter knife for Bat. Bat loved peanut butter, but he could never pack peanut butter sandwiches for school lunches because Lin was allergic to peanuts. The entire Saw Whet School was a nut-free zone.

Janie passed a roll of crackers to Bat.

Mom had heated water in the kettle and poured out three cups of tea.

Tea and crackers and peanut butter. Wonderful.

"I wonder if Stripy will like peanut butter," he said, trying to be casual about the name. "You know, when he's all grown up."

"Stripy?" said Janie. "Is that what you're calling the skunk?"

"It's a good name," Bat said. "It's a really good name. Skunks have stripes."

"I'm not sure it's a good idea to be naming the skunk," Mom said. She looked concerned, with little wavy wrinkles across her squished-up forehead. "If you name him, it will be too easy to get attached. And remember, he's only staying with us for a few more weeks."

"Besides," said Janie, "who says *you* get to name him? I'll bet I could come up with a way better name than Stripy."

"No you couldn't," Bat said, stabbing the knife into the peanut butter jar. "Stripy is the best name for a skunk."

"You always want to give things dumb, obvious names," Janie said.

Bat felt sharp hot tears in his eyes. "Do not," he whispered.

"When you were four, you named your teddy bear Beary. And last year, when that stray cat kept coming into our yard, you named her Patches."

"She was a calico," Bat said. "Calicos look like they are covered in patches."

"Janie," said Mom. "Be nice."

"Aw, Bat doesn't mind, do you, Bat?" asked Janie.

Of course Bat minded. But he didn't want Janie to know how much she had hurt his feelings. "Well, what would *you* name the kit?" he asked.

"I don't know. Give me a minute to think about it."

Janie munched on crackers, and Mom sipped her tea, but Bat just waited to hear what Janie would come up with. He knew it wouldn't be as good as Stripy, and he couldn't wait to tell her so.

"I've got it," Janie said after a minute. "Mom, he was born last Thursday, right?"

"Mm-hmm," Mom said.

"And we want him to be big and strong. We're learning about mythology in school. I think we should name the skunk after the biggest, strongest Nordic god. We should name him Thor."

"Thor?" asked Mom.

"The thunder god," Janie said. "It's perfect, see, because they used to celebrate Thor's day, and now we call that Thursday. And that's when the skunk was born."

"Thor," Bat whispered.

Sometimes, Janie was annoying. Sometimes, she was a mean tease.

But sometimes, Bat thought, she was brilliant.

CHAPTER 14
Sleeping Arrangements

"I want to sleep on the couch. Next to Thor."

"No, Bat, you need to sleep in your own bed," said Mom.

"Then I want Thor to sleep in bed with me."

"You can't sleep with the skunk, Bat. What if you rolled over in the night and crushed him?"

"I would never do that," Bat said. He never would.

"Bat, honey, the skunk—"

"Thor," interrupted Bat. "His name is Thor."

Mom rubbed her forehead. "Fine," she said. "Thor. Thor can't sleep in your bed. Thor is a wild animal. Wild animals don't sleep in beds."

"But in the wild, Thor wouldn't sleep alone," Bat argued. "He would sleep in a pile with all his brothers and sisters, all cuddled up."

"I'm glad people don't sleep like skunks," Janie said. Her hair was damp from the shower, and she was wearing her favorite pajamas, the ones with all the unicorns. Each unicorn was doing something different; one rocked out with a guitar, another was reading a book, another wore a chef's hat and was flipping eggs in a pan. The only thing they had in common was that they were all unicorns.

"Janie, did you know that a herd of unicorns is called a blessing?" Bat asked.

"Yes, Bat, of course I know that. Every time I wear these pajamas you tell me that."

"I didn't know if you remembered," Bat said.

"You're not the only one who remembers things, Bat," said Janie, and then she stomped off to her room.

Bat turned back to Mom. "Pleeeease," he begged.

"No," said Mom in her firm voice. But Bat knew Mom's firm voice. Sometimes, if he pushed hard enough, he could change it into her soft voice, the one that let him have his way.

"I could be the one to feed him, and you could sleep all night," Bat said. "I know how to do it."

"Who do you think took care of you when you were a baby and had to eat every two hours, Bat?" Mom asked. "I took care of you and Janie. I can take care of one little skunk."

"If you let me help," Bat said, bargaining now, "I'll promise to scrape all the extra food off my plate from now on and put it in the dishwasher after dinner."

Mom smiled. "I thought it was too gross to look

at leftover food stuck to a plate."

"It is too gross," Bat said. "But I'll do it anyway." Even if it made him gag. Even if it made him throw up. "Besides," Bat said, "I helped Thor go to the bathroom after he finished eating. If I can do that, I can do other gross things."

Mom had taught Bat that baby skunks don't know how to go to the bathroom on their own when they are little babies. And if they don't pee and poop, they can die. In nature, their mother would help them learn, but since Thor was an orphan, every time he drank his formula someone had to hold him up and rub his bottom with a wet cotton swab until he pooped and peed.

At school, Bat had been helping to clean up Babycakes's enclosure for a while now, and poop and pee were just part of having an animal.

"I'll tell you what, little Bat," Mom said, and her voice was softer now. "Thor has to sleep in his enclosure. And I'm going to take care of him during the night. But you can be in charge of his daytime feedings when we are home. And tomorrow after school, instead of staying home with Janie, how about you come by the clinic? I'm going to weigh and measure Thor to make sure he's getting enough to eat, and you can help."

"Okay," said Bat. "For now. But when Thor gets bigger, big enough that I couldn't squish him in bed, let's revisit this conversation."

That was something Mom said when she wanted Bat to know that they weren't done talking about something, and Bat wanted Mom to know that he wasn't giving up on sleeping with Thor.

Mom laughed. "You drive a hard bargain," she said. "And don't think I'm going to forget about the dishes."

CHAPTER 15
Dr. Jerry Dragoo

Later, in his room when he was supposed to be sleeping, Bat climbed out of bed and pulled his animal encyclopedia from the shelf. He flipped to the *S* section and found the page labeled "Skunk."

At the top of the page was a glossy picture of a large black-and-white skunk nosing along a patch of dirt. In the background of the picture were hundreds of white and yellow daisies.

Below the picture were a bunch of questions and answers about skunks.

Why do skunks spray?

Skunks spray an oily liquid from glands underneath their tails as a defense. Their spray doesn't cause any real damage, but boy, is it stinky! A skunk's smell can be detected by a human from a mile away.

Where do skunks live?

Skunks can make many places their home— abandoned burrows constructed by other animals, a hollow log, even underneath your house!

What are skunks' predators?

Lots of mammals—including red foxes, coyotes, and domestic dogs—will attack a skunk if they get hungry enough, though only as a last resort, because it's difficult to attack a skunk without a smelly reminder of it. But aerial predators—large birds, like owls—don't care so much about the scent. For one thing, it's hard for a skunk to spray at an attacker from the sky. For another, many birds of prey have little to no sense of smell.

Finally, Bat got to the last and most important question.

Do skunks make good pets?
Skunks are wild animals, and wild animals belong in the wild. But according to world skunk expert Dr. Jerry Dragoo, head of the Dragoo Institute for the Betterment of Skunks and Skunk Reputations, while skunks in general do not make good pets, what makes a good pet is a good pet caretaker.

Bat closed the book. He put it back on the shelf, right where he always put it, next to his Lego pyramid. Dr. Jerry Dragoo, world skunk expert. Bat liked that name. He liked doctors, because they usually knew lots of useful things. He liked the name Jerry, because it was the same as that funny mouse in the old cartoons, the one who always outsmarted the cat. And "Dragoo" reminded him of "Dragon." Of course, there was probably no such thing as dragons, but there *might* be.

Dr. Jerry Dragoo. That was someone Bat would like to meet.

CHAPTER 16
A Correspondence

The next day, when it was time for recess, Israel stopped at Bat's desk instead of going outside with the rest of the class and asked, "Hey, Bat, do you want to play Four Square or something?"

"No," said Bat. He was still sitting at his desk.

"No, you don't want to play Four Square?"

"No, I don't want to play anything," Bat answered. All the other kids had left the classroom, and Bat really wanted Israel to leave, too, so that he could talk to Mr. Grayson in private. But Israel kept standing there like he was waiting for something.

"Well, do you want to go outside and just not play anything?"

"No," Bat said. "I don't."

Israel stood next to the desk for a moment longer, sort of smiling, like he was waiting for Bat to say something more. But what could he be waiting for Bat to say? In his head, Bat ran through the list of things that he was supposed to remember to say to people:

Excuse me

I'm sorry

Please

May I

Thank you

"Thank you," Bat said.

"Umm . . . okay," said Israel, and he shrugged, and then, finally, he left.

After Israel was gone, Bat went up to Mr. Grayson's desk. Mr. Grayson had a stack of their current events assignments in front of him, and he was making comments on each one in a green felt-tipped pen.

"Mr. Grayson," Bat said. "I need your help."

Mr. Grayson put the cap on his pen and set it down. "I'm all ears," he said.

That was a funny expression, and for a second Bat pictured Mr. Grayson made entirely of ears, with ears for eyes and an ear for a nose and two tiny rows of little ears for teeth.

"Well," said Bat, "let me tell you about Thor."

And then Bat told Mr. Grayson everything about the skunk kit—about how Mom had brought him home after his mother had died, about how he drank puppy formula because there is no skunk formula, about how he went to the bathroom and how he needed to eat every two hours and how when Mom first brought him home he was almost all pink but now his black fur was starting to grow in and, most of all, how Bat loved him.

"He sounds pretty great," Mr. Grayson said.

"Yes," said Bat. "He is more than pretty great. He is all the way great."

"So how can I help you, Bat?"

"There's a world skunk expert named Dr. Jerry Dragoo. And I want to ask his advice about something. It's important."

"Okay," said Mr. Grayson. He pushed the stack of papers to one side and pulled his laptop from his satchel. He opened it and logged on.

That was one of the great things about Mr. Grayson. If you said you needed help, he just helped without a lot of annoying questions.

"There's only one Dr. Jerry Dragoo," said Mr. Grayson. "He's a professor at a university. We can write him an email, if you want. That's his email address, right there."

Could it really be this easy? Could Bat really just write to the skunk expert? Bat liked to send emails; he sent emails every month to his grand-mother who lived in Idaho, because he hated talking on the phone. Emails gave you time to think. "Okay," said Bat.

"What do you want it to say? I can type for you." Mr. Grayson clicked on his email icon and typed in the address.

"That's all right," said Bat. "I like to type."

Mr. Grayson let Bat sit in his chair.

Bat typed:

Dear Dr. Jerry Dragoo,

Mr. Grayson said, "You can just write 'Dear Dr. Dragoo.' People don't usually use a person's first and last name when they start a letter."

"People don't usually have a name as cool as Dr. Jerry Dragoo," Bat said.

Mr. Grayson laughed. "Can't argue with that."
Bat went on:

My mom brought home a baby skunk. She is a
vet and she had to help him be born. His mother
died, but she didn't have any diseases, and neither
does he. His name is Thor. I want to keep him
as a pet, because I know I can be a good pet
caretaker. Even if I can't keep him forever, I want
to at least keep him until he goes back home to
the wild, not give him to the skunk rescue people.
Please write back and say I can so I can tell my
mom that a world skunk expert says yes. Then she
will probably let me keep him.

"Is that okay?" Bat asked.
Mr. Grayson didn't answer right away, so Bat
turned to look at him. Mr. Grayson's face was

squinched up like he was trying not to laugh, or maybe like he was going to cry.

"Mr. Grayson?" Bat asked. "What's wrong?"

"Nothing is wrong, Bat. That's a very nice email. I will be interested to hear what Dr. Dragoo says."

"Me too," said Bat.

At the end of the email he typed:

Sincerely,

Bixby Alexander Tam (People call me Bat.)

CHAPTER 17
At the Clinic

Bat loved going to Mom's veterinary clinic. If it were up to him, he would go with her every time she had to work late instead of staying home with Janie. But Mom said that as much as she loved having Bat at work with her, all his questions sometimes kept the vet techs from doing their jobs.

Bat *tried* not to ask so many questions. But there

were so many interesting things to ask questions about.

"Today you can help Laurence with baths," Mom told Bat as she drove him the three miles from the Saw Whet School to the small brick building marked "Valerie Tam, DVM."

Janie was always trying to get Mom to rename her veterinary clinic something else. "Something fun," she'd say. "Something creative."

So far, she had suggested the Furry Friends Clinic, Paws for a Moment Veterinarian, Nose to Tail and Everything In Between, and—her favorite—the Pawspital.

But Bat liked seeing Mom's name on the side of the building. It was like she was a celebrity.

"I'm good at baths," Bat said.

"Yes," said Mom. "You are."

When he pulled open the heavy glass door at the

front of the brick building, Bat was overwhelmed by smells and sounds. The lavender-peppermint spray they used to clean up pet accidents. The wet-dog scent of shampooing going on in the back room. Barking, barking, barking. A phone ringing. People talking. A cat's yowl.

If there were this much ruckus at school or the playground or anywhere else at all, Bat would definitely need his earmuffs. But here, the sounds and the smells didn't bother him. Even the flickering fluorescent light didn't irritate him very much.

Suzanne stood behind the counter running a lady's credit card through the machine with one hand while she answered the ringing phone with the other. "Dr. Tam's office," she said, waving hello at Bat as he walked by.

He waved back, but he didn't say anything because he didn't want to bother her. It used to be that he didn't notice if people were busy with other things, but he was way better now. At least, he usually was.

An old lady, old like a grandmother, sat on the bench in the waiting room. She held a box on her lap.

Bat stopped in front of her. "What kind of animal do you have in that box?"

"It's my cat, Pickles," the lady said. "He's not feeling one hundred percent."

"What are his symptoms?" Bat asked.

"Are you the veterinarian?" the lady asked.

"No," said Bat. "Not yet."

"Ah," said the lady. "Well, he has indigestion and he hasn't been very hungry lately."

There were lots of things that could be. Bat looked up at his mom, who stood next to him, listening. She shrugged. "I'll have to examine

Pickles to know what's wrong," she said. Then she turned to the lady. "I'll see you and Pickles in just a minute or two."

"I hope Pickles feels better soon," Bat said. Then he followed Mom through the door that separated the waiting room from the back and watched as she took her white coat from its hook. She put it on, and then Mom was Dr. Tam. A veterinarian. Better than a superhero.

One day, Bat would also have a jacket, just like Mom's. It would be white, and it would have five buttons, and it would have the words "Dr. Tam, DVM" embroidered just above his heart. Of this, Bat was 99.9 percent sure, because that was as sure as you could be about anything.

"I've got to go see patients," Mom said. "You stay close to Laurence, and be a help, okay?"

"Hey, Bat Boy, what's up?" Laurence was the

only person who called Bat "Bat Boy."

"Mom rescued a skunk kit and we're raising it. She says we have to give him to a rescue in a month—well, three weeks now—but I am going to change her mind. We named him Thor," Bat said.

Laurence laughed. "I know all about the kit," he said. "Who do you think is taking care of him while you're at school?"

"You are," said Bat. "Are you doing a good job?"

Laurence rumpled Bat's hair, and Bat smoothed it down again.

"Of course I'm doing a good job," Laurence said. "It's the only kind of job I know how to do. Look." He reached into the neck of his shirt and pulled out the strangest necklace Bat had ever seen. It was made of T-shirt material and ended in a little pouch just big enough for cradling a skunk kit.

"Is Thor in there?" Bat asked.

Laurence nodded. "Yep. The little guy seemed kind of lonely in the kennel, so I made a sling for him out of one of my old T-shirts last night. See? Snug as a bug in a rug." Laurence opened the pouch so Bat could see inside. There was Thor, curled into a little sleeping ball.

"Can I wear him?" Bat asked.

"Of course. We don't want to get him wet when I'm washing the dogs. Here." Very carefully, Laurence pulled the sling up over his head and then lowered it over Bat's. But the sling, which had barely reached Laurence's chest, sank all the way to Bat's belly button.

"We can fix that," said Laurence, and he looped the fabric into a knot behind Bat's neck to shorten the sling. "There," he said. "Now you're a marsupial Bat."

"There are no marsupial bats," Bat said. "Marsupial infants need to have strong arms and claws to climb into their mother's pouch. Bats have wings." Bat peered into the pouch to see if Thor had been disturbed by the movement, but the kit was still fast asleep. "He's got more fur than he had this morning," Bat said. "I can see the black and white growing in."

"They grow up so fast," Laurence said. "You seem bigger than last time I saw you, too."

"Not you," said Bat, closing up the pouch and tucking it into his shirt. "You're already all the way big."

Laurence grinned. "If I get any bigger, I'll have to buy special-order shoes. I already wear the biggest size the shoe store sells."

"Good thing you're too old to grow," Bat said.

"Good thing indeed," said Laurence. Then he said, "Thor is a great name, Bat. Did you come up with it?"

"No," said Bat. "Janie did."

"You're a lucky kid to have such a creative sister," Laurence said. "Did you thank her?"

"No," said Bat. "Not yet."

"Well, there will be time for that later," Laurence

said. "How about assisting me with some baths?"

Usually, Bat would do just about anything to help Laurence with baths. But now, with Thor in the sling, curled up and asleep . . . "I don't know," Bat said.

"Don't worry about the kit," Laurence said. "You can wear an apron. And I'll do all the soapy stuff."

Laurence draped a green apron around Bat's neck. Bat tried to make sure it wasn't pressing too tight against the sling as Laurence tied the waist strap.

"All good?" Laurence asked.

"I can't tell if Thor is still breathing," Bat said. "Maybe it's too tight."

Laurence untied the strap and Bat took off the apron. He pulled open the sling and peered inside. There was Thor, still tightly curled into a little ball, still fast asleep.

"He's okay," sighed Bat.

Laurence patted Bat's shoulder. "Maybe you can just keep me company today. How does that sound, Bat Boy?"

"Better," said Bat. "I can supervise."

"Good idea," Laurence said. "You can tell me when I use too much soap."

"That's easy," said Bat, following Laurence into the holding room, where dogs waited in separate kennels for their bath. "You always use too much soap."

Bat climbed up on a counter across from the big silver washbasin and watched as Laurence bent down to open the far kennel. He scooped up a shaggy white poodle who didn't look very happy about what was about to happen.

"You're okay, Jeff," Laurence said. He was using his soothing voice—calm and deep.

"Jeff is a funny name for a poodle," Bat said.

"Well, Bat's a funny name for a kid," Laurence answered, setting Jeff into the washbasin before smiling at Bat. Bat smiled back.

Then Laurence got to work, slipping Jeff's head into a restraint so he couldn't jump out of the tub, then turning on the faucet and running his hand under the water to check its temperature before he started spraying down the dog.

"That's a new restraint, isn't it?" Bat asked.

"Good eye," said Laurence. He shut off the water and began massaging shampoo into Jeff's curly pelt. "The other one was getting rusty, so I ordered this new model."

"Is that a suction cup connecting it to the wall?"

"It sure is," said Laurence. "And a strong one, too!" He grabbed ahold of the rope and tugged on it to show Bat how well it was connected to the wall . . . but with a loud *pop*, the suction cup came free.

Jeff didn't waste any time. With an excited *yip*, he scrambled over the lip of the washbasin and leaped to the ground, bubbles everywhere. He slipped and slid when he landed, his nails scraping across the linoleum floor. Laurence reached to grab him, but Jeff was too fast. He scrambled toward the door.

Bat pulled his legs up onto the counter and crossed them, one arm wrapping protectively around Thor in his sling. The air smelled like warm wet dog and strawberry shampoo.

Laurence's fingers were inches away from Jeff when his heel found a puddle of soapy water. One moment he was standing, and the next moment he was flat on his back.

"Are you okay?" Bat asked, but he didn't climb down from his perch. His first priority was keeping the kit safe and dry.

"I've been better," Laurence groaned. Jeff, who had discovered that the door was closed tight, returned to peer down at Laurence. He lowered his head and lovingly licked Laurence's cheek with his long pink tongue.

CHAPTER 18
Dinner Date

Maybe the best moment of the whole day was when Bat finally felt Thor rustling in the pouch that hung from around Bat's neck. Thor woke from his nap just when Laurence was finishing the last bath, which was for an inky spaniel named Webster.

"Laurence!" Bat said. "Thor is waking up!"

Bat pulled open the sling and gently extracted

the kit from it, holding Thor's warm, wiggly body up to his cheek. The kit's nose twitched as he snuffed around.

"Baby wants his milk," Laurence said, and together they fed him.

If Bat had his way, he would wear Thor in the sling all the time. But Mom made him take it off at bath time and bedtime. She was willing to compromise at dinner.

"Really, Bat, don't you think Thor would be more comfortable in his enclosure?" Mom said as she served out three platefuls of spaghetti and meatballs.

"No," said Bat. "I really don't."

Mom squinted her eyes tight. When she opened them she said, "Okay. Thor can join us for dinner. As long as he stays in the sling."

"I'll bet when he's older, though, Thor will

love spaghetti and meatballs," Bat said happily,
twirling a messy forkful of noodles. "Skunks eat
everything, you know. They're omnivores. *Omni*,
meaning everything, *vore*, meaning one who eats."

"We *know*, Bat," said Janie. "You told us already.
Like a hundred times."

"Don't you think it's interesting?" asked Bat.

"Don't I think *what* is interesting?"

"Everything," said Bat. "Everything there is to know about animals."

"Not really," said Janie. "I think theater is way more interesting than animals."

"That's stupid," said Bat. Because it was.

"Bat," said Mom in her warning voice. Deep and serious, with her eyebrows pointed toward her nose.

"I'm sorry I said your interest is stupid," said Bat. He wasn't actually sorry, because Janie's interest *was* stupid. Theater was pretend. Animals were real. But Mom had let him bring Thor to the dinner table, so Bat turned his mouth up in a smile and added, "Will you forgive me?" Mom liked it when he remembered to say that.

"Whatever," Janie said. "Mom, did you make any garlic bread?"

"Oh, it's in the oven. It's probably done," Mom said.

Janie pushed back from the table, found an oven mitt in the drawer, and pulled the tray of bread out of the oven. It smelled wonderful.

"Ezra once said that garlic is the best smell in the world, better even than roses," Janie said, putting the bread slices into a basket and bringing it to the table.

"That Ezra is a character," Mom said.

"He's pretty funny," Janie said. "He even makes our math teacher laugh, and she doesn't think *anything* is funny."

"If she doesn't think anything is funny," Bat said, reaching across the table for a piece of bread, "then why does she laugh at Ezra? Is it mean laughing?"

"No, Bat," said Janie. "She thinks Ezra is funny."

"Then why did you say she doesn't think *anything* is funny?"

"Never mind, Bat," said Janie.

Bat took bite of the garlic bread. The crust was crusty, and then the inside was hot and squishy. Melted butter glazed his fingers, which he licked, one by one.

They ate for a few minutes without talking, the only sounds the crunch of biting into bread and the scraping noise of forks against plates as they wound bites of spaghetti.

Then, Janie announced, "I've decided I'm going to audition for the Queen."

"I thought you wanted to be Alice," Mom said.

"That was before I read the script," Janie said. "Then I realized that Alice is boring. She just wanders around whining about everything."

"You'd be good at that part," Bat said. "You're good at whining."

"Mo-o-m," whined Janie. "Make him stop!"

"Bat," said Mom. "That wasn't nice."

"But I said she'd make a good Alice," Bat said.

"But not for a good reason," Mom explained.

"Why does the reason matter? I gave her a compliment."

"I don't think it felt like a compliment to Janie," Mom said. "Janie, did it feel like a compliment to you?"

"No," said Janie. "It was an insult."

"You see, Bat?" said Mom. "It wasn't a compliment to Janie."

Suddenly Bat wished that he had been wearing his earmuffs and that he hadn't even heard Mom and Janie talking about the play. Sometimes it was just better if Bat kept his thoughts to himself.

Bat ate a few more bites of his spaghetti and had almost finished all his bread when he felt Thor wriggling around in his pouch. "May I be excused?" he asked.

"Yes," said Janie.

"Honey, you know it's up to you to model good behavior," Bat heard Mom say to Janie as he headed to the refrigerator to get out the puppy formula.

"Sometimes, Mom, even I'm not a good enough actress to pretend not to notice when Bat is being weird."

"Oh, Janie," said Mom.

Get out the formula, Bat told himself. Put some in the syringe. Warm it up. Ignore Janie.

Bat knew that sometimes Janie thought he was weird. But he still didn't like to hear her say it out loud.

Actually, Janie could be weird, too. Like when she sang at the top of her lungs in the shower, even though there wasn't an audience. And how she cared if her hair was wavy or straight. Did

Ezra ever think that Janie was weird? Maybe that's what makes Ezra her friend, Bat thought. He likes the parts of her that everyone else thinks are weird.

CHAPTER 19
A Blessing of Sorts

Five nights later, at bedtime, Janie noticed the nice thing that Bat had done to thank her for coming up with the perfect name for Thor. It had taken him two days to forgive Janie for being so mean during spaghetti night and another day to come up with an idea. He'd been waiting ever since for Janie to notice, so when she called out from her bedroom, "Mom, have you seen the top part of my unicorn pajamas?" Bat felt excited.

"I did all the laundry that was in the basket," Mom answered.

"You washed the bottoms but not the top," Janie said.

"Then you must not have put the top in the laundry basket."

"Why would I put in the bottoms but not the top?" Janie asked.

"Why would I wash just the bottoms if the top was in the basket, too?" Mom asked back.

Then it was time for Bat to reveal the nice thing. "I know where your unicorn pajama top is," he said.

"You do?" said Mom and Janie together.

"Yes," Bat said. "I took it out of the dirty laundry basket."

"Why would you do that?" Mom asked.

"Because if I waited until after you washed it, then Thor wouldn't recognize Janie's scent."

Janie had been the one to name Thor. Even though Bat didn't like the idea of sharing Thor with anyone, Janie had earned the right for Thor to know who she was.

"Did you give that rodent my pajama top?" Janie's voice climbed higher and higher.

"Actually," Bat said, "skunks aren't rodents. They're Mephitidae. People used to think that they belonged in the same family as weasels, ferrets, and badgers, but this scientist named Dr. Jerry Dragoo figured out that—"

"It doesn't *matter*, Bat," Janie said, interrupting him. "Go get my pajama top *right now*."

"But it *does* matter," said Bat.

Janie was not interested in hearing the difference between Mephitidae and Mustelidae. She refused to listen to anything until after Bat had gone to Thor's enclosure and retrieved the unicorn pajama top from the pile where Thor slept. And when he tried to hand it to her, she wouldn't even take it.

"It smells like animal," she said.

"It smelled like animal before, too," Bat said. "Because I took it from the dirty laundry basket, and it still smelled like you."

She didn't *scream*, exactly. Bat didn't know what to call the sound that she made just before she spun around, stomped back into her room, and slammed the door.

Bat felt tears gathering, ready to spill. Mom came over and hugged him tight. She didn't say anything, but she rocked him back and forth in the way he liked, and after a moment Bat felt the sting of his tears begin to fade.

"It was a nice gesture," Mom murmured into his hair. Bat liked the hot warmth of her breath.

"Baby skunks are easier than sisters," Bat said.

"That may be true," Mom answered. "But there are lots of baby skunks in the world, and you only have one sister."

Gently, she took Janie's pajama top from Bat's hand. He hadn't realized that he was still clutching it. "Come on," she said. "I'll teach you how to do laundry."

"Okay," said Bat. "But first I need to check one thing." He stuck his head into Thor's enclosure to make sure the kit was settled back in after having his nest disturbed. Thor was sleeping soundly, making a noise like a tiny little snore. Bat pulled one of his own T-shirts up over Thor's body, tucking him in. Then he latched the enclosure and followed Mom to the laundry room.

"Maybe if we use extra fabric softener," he said, "and make the pajama top softer than it's ever been, then maybe Janie won't be so mad."

"I think that is a very good idea," Mom said. "And you can pour it in."

CHAPTER 20
Problems

"Earth to Bat," Mr. Grayson said.

Bat looked up. He had been staring at his math work in front of him, but he hadn't been doing the problems. Usually, Bat liked math problems, because he was good at them and they made sense. Usually, Bat asked for extra math problems when he was done with his regular math problems. But today, Bat didn't feel like doing the regular math problems, even though they were easy. Today, all

Bat could think about was that time was passing very quickly, and that he still hadn't heard back from Dr. Jerry Dragoo, world skunk expert.

"You look like you're having a hard time focusing today, Bat," said Mr. Grayson.

"I'm not having a hard time focusing," said Bat.

"Let me rephrase that. You look like you're having a hard time focusing *on your schoolwork* today, Bat."

"Yes," said Bat. "I am focused on something else."

"He can't think about anything other than that stupid baby skunk," said Lucca.

"Thor isn't stupid," Bat said. He felt his throat grow tight with anger.

"Once my dog got sprayed by a skunk when we were camping," Israel said. "He was stinky for a week."

"Okay, okay," said Mr. Grayson. "This is all very

interesting, but right now is math time. Not skunk time."

There *should* be skunk time at school, thought Bat. He picked up his pencil and forced his brain to focus on the math problems. Most of them were too easy to even bother working out on paper, but he showed all the steps because Mr. Grayson liked it when he showed his work, and Bat liked Mr. Grayson.

While part of Bat's brain worked with his hand to do the math work, he let another part of his brain think about skunk time. If there were a skunk time at school, like math time and language arts time and yoga time, then maybe Bat could bring Thor with him. Maybe skunk time would be when everyone in class did research about skunks and wrote reports about skunks and built skunk dioramas.

Over the last week, Bat had spent as much time as he could with Thor, but every day he had to leave him when it was time for school. The kit's fur was growing in all over, fuzzy wild black hair with a bright white stripe down the center, from the tip of his nose to the tip of his tail. He was still small enough to fit, curled into a little ball, in Bat's two hands.

And he'd had plenty of time to spend with Thor, because Janie had barely spoken to him since the pajama-top incident. She spent all her time in her room practicing the "Off with Her Head" song for her Queen audition and going over to Ezra's house. Now an Every-Other Friday was coming, and Bat would have to go with Janie to Dad's house. Even worse, no matter how much Bat begged and pleaded and bounced up and down, no matter how clearly he explained to Mom why she should change her mind, Thor would not be going to Dad's house with Bat and Janie. This Every-Other Friday meant that Thor had already spent two weeks living with Bat and his family, and if Bat didn't find a way to change Mom's mind, in two more weeks, Thor would be leaving for the rescue center.

"Thor will be fine, Bat," Mom had said. "Laurence

is going to take him for the weekend."

It wasn't that Laurence couldn't do a good job of taking care of animals, Bat thought as he finished the last row of math problems. It wasn't that Bat didn't *trust* Laurence. It was just that . . . well, Bat didn't want anyone else taking care of the skunk kit. What if Laurence did a better job? What if Thor was happier at Laurence's house than at their house?

And, even if Laurence was trustworthy, no one was perfect. What if Laurence put the animal carrier on the top of his car while he unlocked the door, and then he forgot it was up there and he drove away? What if Laurence went out to get some ice cream and didn't remember to lock the door to his house and someone broke into it and stole Thor? Even if everything went just right, at the end of the weekend they would be two days closer to Thor leaving them forever. Just thinking about that made Bat feel queasy, like he'd been jumping on a trampoline with a stomach full of pizza.

"Bat," said Mr. Grayson. "Do you need to take a little break?"

Bat stopped tapping his heels under the table. He pulled the neck of his T-shirt, which he'd been sucking on in the way he sometimes did when he felt nervous, out of his mouth. He set his pencil down.

"Yes, please," he said.

In the back of the room, Babycakes sat placidly licking a light-pink wheel of salt. Her ears flopped to the sides in relaxation.

Bat wished he felt as calm as Babycakes looked. He climbed into her enclosure and sat cross-legged beside her, scratching behind her ears and thinking about the weekend.

If his parents weren't divorced, then he wouldn't have to leave home every other weekend and go to his dad's dumb apartment. If his parents weren't divorced, Thor wouldn't be spending the weekend with Laurence.

CHAPTER 21
Organizational Systems

At least Dad liked to go to the candy store as much as Bat did. That was one good thing about Every-Other Weekends.

On Saturday morning, after breakfast and dishes, Dad pulled their bicycles out of his garage. Unlike the garage at home, which was twice as big and four times as crowded, Dad's garage was labeled and organized. Helmets were kept in a clear plastic bin marked "Helmets." The bikes, instead of leaning up against a wall or on each other, were pulled neatly into a bike rack like the one at school, and Dad always arranged them in order of size, left to right: large, medium, small.

A metal rack in one corner held car supplies—spare containers of oil, a big jug of windshield wiper fluid, a little vacuum that sat ready on its charger.

There was a tool bench, too. An assortment of wrenches swung from hooks across the front. Coffee cans held screws and nails. Sometimes Dad let Bat pound nails into pieces of scrap wood, as long as he wore safety goggles.

Bat approved of Dad's garage.

It was just under a one-mile ride to the Sugar Shack, Bat's favorite candy store. To get there, Bat and Janie and Dad rode out of Dad's apartment complex and down a bike path toward central Quincy. They crossed the river on a bridge made just for bicycles and pedestrians before turning onto Third Street.

While Bat was double-checking the lock on his bike outside the Sugar Shack, he heard someone say his name. It was Israel, from school. It took Bat a second to figure out who he was, because Bat hadn't ever seen Israel anywhere but at school, and never on a weekend.

"What are you doing here?" Israel asked. He was smiling in a way that showed almost all his teeth. He had, Bat noticed, a piece of something green—maybe cucumber—stuck in between the two front teeth.

"We're going to buy some candy," Bat said.

"Cool," Israel said. Then he said, "We just had brunch next door," and he pointed to the Broken Yolk Café. A man and woman were pushing through the door just then, and they waved. Israel waved back.

"That's what I would have guessed," Bat said. "You have food in your teeth."

Israel's smile fell away.

"Okay," said Bat. "See you Monday at school."

"Hey," said Israel. "Wait."

Bat waited.

"I was wondering about the skunk. Do you still have him?"

"Of course I do," said Bat. Then, "Well, not right now. Because I had to spend the weekend with my dad."

"Oh," said Israel. "I didn't know your parents were divorced."

Bat didn't say anything to that, because it wasn't a question. Still, Israel stood there, on the sidewalk, like he was waiting for Bat to say something. The grown-ups who had waved at Israel walked over and stood behind him, and now it felt like all three of them were waiting for Bat to say something, or to do something.

"Well, good-bye," Bat said, and he walked away.

"Hey, sport, is that a friend from school?" Dad's face looked just about as excited as it looked when he was watching baseball.

"Bat doesn't have friends," Janie said, but not in a mean voice, just a matter-of-fact voice.

"I'm sure that's not true," Dad said.

"It's not true," Bat answered. "Laurence is my friend. And Mr. Grayson."

"Oh, Bat, grown-ups don't count," Janie said. Then she pulled open the door to the candy store and held it for Bat to pass inside.

The Sugar Shack was an exceptional candy store. It had bins full of M&M's separated into colors, so if you wanted exactly eleven greens and eleven blues, but no yellows, reds, or oranges (as Bat did), you could get exactly that.

Along the back wall were all the gummies— gummy bears, gummy worms, gummy sharks. Gummy hippos, gummy rhinos, gummy jellyfish. Gummy dinosaurs. Gummy frogs. Gummy sea stars. Gummy zebras, gummy camels, gummy parrots. Gummy crabs.

Bat didn't like gummy candy, but he always got one gummy sea star anyway. He liked the way they felt in his hand.

Big barrels full of hard candies formed the

aisles. Jawbreakers and gum balls and candy necklaces and rock candy and ring pops. Just inside the door was a case of jelly beans arranged in a rainbow of colors. Near the counter stood a candy-bar display, with all the ordinary stuff but harder-to-find candy bars, too, like Violet Crumble bars and Zagnut bars.

"You sure inherited my sweet tooth," Dad said, loading up his own plastic bag with jelly beans.

"Actually," Bat said, "teeth have nothing to do with it. People taste with their tongues and their noses."

"Do you stick that gummy bear up your nose to taste it?" Janie asked. Her bag was full of a mish-mash of candies that didn't make any sense to Bat.

"It's a gummy sea star," Bat said. "And no. The way something smells is part of how you taste it."

"Well, I guess that's why people don't eat skunk

meat," Janie said. "*Pe-ew.*" She wrinkled up her nose and stuck out her tongue.

"Thor doesn't stink," Bat said. "He doesn't even spray yet."

"But he will," Janie said. "I hope not until after we give him to the rescue."

"Maybe we'll keep him," Bat whispered.

"Sport, your mom can't adopt every stray animal that comes into her clinic," Dad said. "She'd have a zoo if she did."

"We won't adopt *all* of them," Bat said. "Just this one."

"Mom said we're only going to keep him for a couple more weeks," Janie told Dad. "But Bat is getting too attached."

Bat started bouncing on the balls of his feet. He clutched his plastic candy bag in his fist. It crinkled in a way that bothered his ears, so he loosened his fingers and let it go.

Blue and green M&M's bounced and rolled across the floor of the Sugar Shack.

"Sport, you've got to be more careful," Dad said, his eyebrows pointing in at his nose. Bat felt tears welling up in his eyes. He swiped at his face with the arm of his shirt and turned toward the door. Under the sole of his shoe, he felt the crunch-squish of a flattened M&M.

CHAPTER 22
Baseball and Braiding

Before bed on Sunday night, Janie always took a shower and washed her hair. Lately, she'd been weaving it into six braids while it was still damp so that she could have wavy hair in the morning.

Janie's hair was usually stick-straight, like Dad's and Bat's, though hers was a dark, dark brown instead of black.

When she came out of the bathroom in her

pajamas carrying a wide-tooth comb and six hair ties, Bat asked, "Can I braid it?"

"I can do it myself," Janie said.

"Let him try," Dad said from the couch, where he sat watching baseball on TV. He had an orange-and-black baseball cap on his head because tonight he was rooting for the Orioles. He had a collection of caps for all the teams he liked, and whenever one of his teams was playing, he'd select the right baseball cap from the top shelf in his closet and wear it for the whole game.

Dad said he didn't believe in luck, but it sort of seemed like he did.

"Okay," said Janie. "But if you mess up the braids, I'm going to redo them."

She sat cross-legged on the floor facing the TV. Bat sat behind her on the couch next to Dad. Janie handed him the comb.

Bat started combing at the bottom, the way

Janie had taught him, so he wouldn't pull her hair. He worked out all the little tangles with the teeth of the comb as he made his way up toward the top of her head. Soon he could pull the comb straight through her hair, from the very top to the ends, without snagging at all.

Then he divided her hair into six sections: two in the front, two in the middle, and two in the back. The back two sections looked a little thicker than the others, but Bat didn't think Janie would notice. He picked up the front left section of hair and started braiding.

"Go, go, go!" Dad yelled at the TV. One of the baseball players had made a good hit and was running as fast as he could around the bases.

"I think baseball is the most boring game you watch," Janie said. "Even more boring than football."

"That's because you won't let me explain it to

you," Dad said, adjusting his cap. "If you under-
stand the game, it's fascinating."

Bat reached the bottom of the first section of
hair and wound a pink elastic band around its
end. The braid wasn't perfectly neat and straight
like the braids Janie did, but it wasn't bad. Moving
on to the other front section, Bat focused on making the second braid even better than the first.

"Make sure you're braiding it tight," Janie said, "so it's really wavy."

"I am," Bat said.

Bat loved braiding Janie's hair, even though he usually wasn't very good at hand things. He liked the feeling of the damp, heavy hair; he liked organizing it into a series of smaller, neatly contained braids; he liked feeling close to Janie like this, by helping her and touching her, without having to have a big conversation that might turn into a fight.

Getting along with people was hard for Bat. Figuring out what they meant when they said something, or when they made certain faces at him . . . People were complicated. But braiding was easy.

There. He'd finished the second braid and wrapped the end of this one in a dark-green elastic.

Janie reached up and touched the braid, then pulled it in front of her face so she could see it. "Not bad," she said.

"Yes!" yelled Dad. He stood up from the couch, grabbing the cap from his head and waving it around.

It wasn't the same as being at home. Mom wasn't here. Thor wasn't here. But maybe Every-Other Weekends could be okay.

CHAPTER 23
Windows

Some days, Bat was the first person awake. It didn't happen often because Mom was a morning person. Usually when Bat woke up, he went straight into the kitchen to find Mom sitting at the table with a cup of coffee and a book. But every now and then, Bat awoke to a completely quiet house. A sleeping house.

Tuesday was one of those mornings. Bat woke

up, suddenly and completely, to a still-dark sky outside his window. He blinked and sat up, slipped his feet into his slippers, took the skunk sling from the doorknob where he'd hung it the night before, and went into the living room.

The living room windows faced the front yard. Bat could make out the shape of the big oak tree on the lawn. It was a darker shadow against the velvety early-morning sky.

He went straight to Thor's enclosure and found the kit tucked in his sleeping corner, surrounded by the rice-filled socks that made a nice padded nook. He stroked Thor's back, feeling the rise and fall of his sleeping breaths, before gently scooping him up. Thor let out a little high-pitched yawning sound, his tiny paws swimming through the air as Bat settled him into the sling. Once inside, Thor rustled around for a moment before quieting back down.

In the kitchen, Bat opened the refrigerator as quietly as he could and retrieved the formula. He filled the syringe and held it under a stream of hot water to warm it up. Thor could smell the formula; Bat could tell because he wriggled around in his pouch.

"It's coming, little guy," Bat said. When the formula was warm he went back into the living room and curled up on the window bench. Already, the sky was changing. It was still dark, but now Bat could make out the branches of the tree. He heard the very earliest morning birds, the ones that sang each day as the sky began to lighten.

Gently, Bat reached into the pouch and pulled out the skunk kit. It was too dark to see clearly, but Bat didn't want to startle him by turning on a lamp, so he brought the syringe down to Thor's face and let the skunk find the tip by smell.

As Thor had his breakfast, the sky turned

violet and pink, then orangey red. The tree's trunk lightened from black to brown and its leaves transformed to green. The first birds called louder, waking up their friends, and they became a chorus of song.

Bat looked down to see if Thor had finished his formula and gasped in surprise. The two tight slits that had been closed since Mom first brought him home were open. Bat could see Thor's eyes.

They were the darkest black Bat had ever seen.

"Hey there," Bat cooed down at Thor. "Good morning, little kit."

Thor kept licking at the tip of the syringe, but his quick pink tongue hesitated just a bit when Bat spoke. Maybe he was listening! Maybe he understood.

Bat stroked back the soft black-and-white fuzz

on Thor's little forehead. "I see you!" he said. "Do you see me?"

Mom emerged from her bedroom, tying the belt of her robe. "Bat?" she said. "You're up early."

"Mom!" Bat said. "Look! Thor's eyes are open!"

Mom came over to see. "Look at that," she said, resting her hand on the top of Bat's head and petting his hair, just as Bat stroked Thor.

"His eyes are beautiful, Mom," Bat said. "Don't you think his eyes are beautiful?"

Mom sat down on the window seat next to Bat. "I think that's the first time I've ever heard you mention someone's eyes," she said.

"Most eyes are boring," Bat said. "But Thor's eyes are amazing. Look! They are the color of outer space. They're open!"

"Bat," Mom said, "what color are *my* eyes?"

"Brown," Bat answered, still staring at the

skunk kit. Droplets of formula hung from little black-and-white hairs all around his mouth.

"Nope," said Mom. "They're hazel."

This got Bat's attention. "Really?" He looked up and stared at Mom's face. Her eyes were golden brown with little flecks of green and yellow in them.

"They look like marbles," Bat said. "I never noticed."

"Well, you never have been all that interested in people's eyes."

Bat shrugged. "I never thought about it," he said.

"Some people say you can tell a lot about a person by looking into their eyes," Mom said. "What do you think about that?"

Bat thought about it. "I don't get it," he said. "If I want to know something about a person, I ask. I think you can tell more about people from what they say than from their eyes."

"Hmm," said Mom. "You have an interesting way of seeing the world, Bat."

Bat stared deep into Thor's space-black eyes. He tried to see what he could learn from them. He looked first into the left eye, and then into the right, and then into the left again. "It's hard to look into two eyes at the same time," he said. "Which one am I supposed to look in?"

"I don't think it matters. Try looking into my eyes," Mom said, "and see what you can learn about me."

Bat tucked Thor back into the pouch. Mom took the syringe and set it down. She took Bat's hands into hers and smiled at him.

Bat smiled back, and then he tried to see what Mom's eyes could tell him. The left eye had three more flecks of green than the right eye. The right eye had one more fleck of yellow.

The black points in the middle were exactly the same size. Her eyes were shiny.

"Hazel is cool," Bat said. "It's like a rainbow of all the boring colors."

"Funny Bat," Mom said. "Do you know what I see when I look into your eyes?"

"Brown and black," Bat said. "With white all around."

"Yes," said Mom. "I do see that. But I also see your sweetness. And your thoughtful nature. And your busy, busy mind."

Bat looked away. It was uncomfortable to let anyone look into his eyes for too long. It made him feel kind of itchy and shy. "You can tell all that by looking in my eyes?"

"Yes," she said. She leaned forward and kissed Bat's forehead. "I see all of that and more."

CHAPTER 24
A Reply

"Bat," said Mr. Grayson as the students filed into the classroom. "You got an email from Dr. Jerry Dragoo."

"He wrote back?" Bat said, his heart beating faster. There were only a few days left until Thor was supposed to go to the rescue center, and he had almost given up hope. "What did he say?"

"You can read it at recess," Mr. Grayson said. "It's a nice email."

"I want to read it now." All the other kids were at their desks, but Bat was still standing in the aisle. He felt his hands pull up tight against his sides the way they did when he was excited.

"At recess, Bat," said Mr. Grayson.

Bat hated waiting. He hated, hated waiting. It was stupid to wait for something if there was no good reason that it couldn't happen *now*. Who cared if class started a few minutes late, if it meant that he could read his email? A real-life skunk expert had written to him. That was certainly more important than anything Mr. Grayson had planned right now. Had a real-life skunk expert ever written to Mr. Grayson? Almost certainly not.

"Mr. Grayson, I think you should let me read my email now," Bat said.

"Bat," Mr. Grayson answered, "sometimes we have to wait. It's good practice to delay gratification."

Bat didn't really know what Mr. Grayson meant by that, but he knew it meant that Mr. Grayson wasn't going to let him read the email right now. He wanted to insist, and he would insist if he thought he could change Mr. Grayson's mind. But Mr. Grayson looked serious, so Bat reluctantly went to his seat.

"Too bad," said Israel, putting down the book he had been reading.

"Don't make fun of me!" Bat yelled.

"Whoa, dude," Israel said. "I wasn't making fun of you!"

"Bat," said Mr. Grayson, coming over to his desk. "What on earth is the matter?"

"Israel was making fun of me," Bat said.

"I was not," said Israel. "I just said it's too bad Bat can't read his email right now."

"You don't really think it's too bad," Bat said. He kept his eyes on the surface of his desk, running his gaze over the wood grain.

"You don't know what I think, Bat," said Israel. "You don't know everything."

"Bat," said Mr. Grayson, putting his hand on Bat's shoulder. The weight of his hand felt good. It helped Bat to feel like he was sitting in his seat, like he wasn't going to fly away. "Try to give Israel the benefit of the doubt, okay? If he says he was being sincere, believe him."

Bat nodded, but he didn't look up. Israel went back to his book.

"For what it's worth, Bat," said Mr. Grayson, in a quieter voice, "I think Israel was being kind. I think he'd like to be your friend." Then Mr. Grayson took his hand off Bat's shoulder and returned to the front of the room.

Now Bat wasn't just thinking about the email from Dr. Jerry Dragoo. He was also thinking about whether Israel wanted to be his friend. He thought about how Israel had asked him if he wanted to play Four Square and how he had said hello outside of the Sugar Shack. Then he thought about the other kids in the class looking at him right now, and he thought about Thor's eyes, and he thought about the windy day outside. It was too much to think about all at once, and his skin began to feel prickly and too tight.

But he couldn't take off his skin, so instead he reached into his backpack for his earmuffs and slipped them on. The classroom noise around him faded, and Bat's skin calmed down.

Bat looked at the clock above the classroom door. It was 8:55. Recess was at 10:15. That was exactly one hour and twenty minutes away. He could wait that long. He didn't like it, but he could do it.

Time was a funny thing. Sometimes, an hour and twenty minutes didn't feel very long at all. Like when Bat was watching YouTube videos about animals. And sometimes, like when Dad was watching baseball on TV, an hour and twenty minutes felt like twenty years. But that day, the hour and twenty minutes between 8:55 and 10:15 felt like twenty baseball games.

At last, Mr. Grayson said, "Okay, gang, go play!"

The kids shoved back their chairs and headed for the door. Bat pulled off his earmuffs and went to Mr. Grayson's desk. "It's recess," he said.

"Yes, Bat, it sure is," said Mr. Grayson. He opened his laptop.

"Can I read the email, too?" Israel asked. He hadn't gone outside with the other kids.

"Why?" asked Bat.

"Because I'm curious. You've been talking about Dr. Jerry Dragoo nonstop."

That wasn't true. Was it? Maybe it was true. "Okay," said Bat. "But no making fun."

"I wasn't making fun before," Israel said, "and I won't now."

"Here you go, gentlemen," Mr. Grayson said. He clicked on the top message in his inbox. The subject line was "Re: Question about a Baby Skunk." Then he stood up so that Bat could have his chair. "When you're done reading your email, just close the laptop and come join us outside," he said. Then he headed out to the playground. Bat sat down. He could feel Israel standing behind him, reading over his shoulder.

The email read:

Dear Bat,

I am very interested in skunks, as you know. I can tell that you feel very attached to the kit, and I don't blame you. Baby skunks are adorable! But the question of whether you should keep him as a pet is a complicated one, even if your mom feels reasonably sure that he is disease-free. All pets require a huge commitment of time, energy, and usually, money. Skunks are no different.

In fact, keeping a skunk as a pet is much more challenging than keeping a dog or a cat. Skunks are not pets by nature. They are wild animals. And from my many years of experience, I can tell you that most people don't know what they are getting into.

It's very easy to fall in love with a baby skunk, but it's difficult to truly be a good caretaker to a skunk. Most people would be better off with a dog. Still, this skunk kit has come into your life, and for at least the next few weeks, you and your mother must work to be the best caretakers you can be.

Should you keep the kit? Should you give him to the rescue people? I don't know the answer because I don't know you and I don't know your kit. But it sounds like, for now, the kit is right where it needs to be, and I trust that you will take good care of it.

Sincerely,

Jerry Dragoo, PhD

Dragoo Institute for the Betterment of Skunks and Skunk Reputations

"That's too bad," said Israel.

"What's too bad?" asked Bat.

"That the skunk guy doesn't think you should keep the kit."

"That's not what he said," said Bat.

"Well, he didn't say that he'd tell your mom to keep him. He didn't say that skunks make good pets."

"That's true," said Bat. "But he didn't say we shouldn't keep Thor, either. He said that a good caretaker makes a good pet. So all I have to do is be the best caretaker in the world. And convince my mom to let me keep raising him. I can do that." Bat closed Mr. Grayson's laptop, absolutely determined to become the very best caretaker that a skunk had ever had.

"Can I come over sometime?" Israel asked.

"Why?" said Bat.

"I don't know," said Israel. "To hang out. And maybe meet Thor."

"It's okay with me," Bat answered. "I'll have to ask my mom."

CHAPTER 25
Houseguests

There were just a few days left before Thor was supposed to leave for the animal rescue. Bat didn't have any time to lose, and all afternoon he practiced how he was going to tell Mom about Dr. Jerry Dragoo and how important it was that Thor stay with them as long as possible. But that night at dinner, he found himself nervously avoiding the topic. What if he couldn't change Mom's mind?

Bat couldn't imagine anything worse than that. So instead of telling her about Dr. Jerry Dragoo, Bat said, "Israel wants to come over to our house."

"Who's Israel?" asked Janie, dipping her chicken chunk into barbecue sauce.

"He's a kid in my class," Bat said.

"Bat, honey, that's great!" said Mom.

"Is he your friend?" Janie asked.

Bat considered the question. *Was* Israel his friend? Israel was nice to him. He was interested in some of the same things that interested Bat. He didn't seem to think that Bat was weird. And he wanted to visit.

"I don't know," Bat said. "Maybe he is."

"That's kind of a big deal," said Janie. "You've never had a friend over before."

"Yes I have," Bat said. "Ezra comes over all the time."

"He's *my* friend, not yours," Janie said.

"He can be your friend and Bat's," said Mom.

"I thought you said Ezra is annoying," Janie said.

"He is annoying," said Bat. "But so are you, and you are still my friend."

"No one is more annoying than you," said Janie. "But I guess you're my friend, too."

"Neither of you is annoying," said Mom. "And Bat, I think it's great that you want to have a friend over."

"Well," said Bat, dipping his chicken chunk in ketchup. "It was Israel's idea, not mine. He wants to meet Thor."

At that moment, Thor was just where he should be—tucked into his pouch, warm against Bat's chest. And remembering Thor made Bat nervous all over again.

"I think it's a great idea, no matter whose it was," said Mom. "I'll call Israel's parents to set something up. Maybe Saturday?"

"Whenever," Bat said. And then he said, "Mom, there's something else, too."

"What is it?" Mom had a chicken chunk in her hand, already dipped in sauce, but she set it down.

"I wrote to a world skunk expert," Bat said. The words came out fast and loud, because they were important. "I wrote and asked him about keeping Thor as a pet. Because I don't want to send him to the rescue people. I want to raise him here, at our house. I love Thor. I think maybe he loves me, too. And I'm not ready to give him away."

"Oh, Bat," Mom said. "How on earth did you find a world skunk expert?"

And then Bat told her about reading in his animal encyclopedia about Dr. Jerry Dragoo, and about Mr. Grayson helping him with the email, and about waiting and waiting for a response, and about finally getting an email back, and about how Israel had wanted to read it, too. "I can be a good skunk caretaker, Mom," he said last, and then he waited to hear what she would say.

But it was Janie who spoke. "Wow, Bat," she said. "That's pretty cool, that you found an expert and wrote to him. That takes guts. I think you should let him keep raising the skunk, Mom. He's pretty serious."

Bat was so surprised that he felt his mouth drop open. *Janie* was helping him?

"Bat," Mom said, "I've been watching you with the kit. You are so responsible and careful with him. But honey, raising Thor until he's old enough to release is a big commitment. He'd have to stay with us all through the rest of the school year, and through summer, as well."

That sounded wonderful to Bat. "The longer the better," he said.

"You say that now," Mom said, "but what if you get tired of feeding him and cleaning up after him? And what about when he gets bigger and he's awake more of the time?"

"Mom," said Bat, and he did his very best to make his voice sound as serious as he felt, "I will never get tired of Thor. That would be like you getting tired of me and Janie."

Mom laughed, and she reached over to squeeze Bat's hand. Then she shook her head, which Bat knew was the sign for "no," and he felt his eyes stinging with unspilled tears. But she said, "Beautiful Bat, you have become an excellent skunk caretaker. You have been dedicated, and you even found a way to contact a skunk expert! I have to admit, I am impressed. I'll tell you what: I'm thinking that maybe we won't call the animal rescue center next week, and we can try having you take care of Thor—with my help—until he's old enough to release. How does that sound?"

How did it sound? It sounded not as good as a promise that he could keep Thor forever, but still impossibly good. Bat felt like he was vibrating on the inside, he was so happy. He wanted to jump up and whoop with joy, but Thor was curled up and asleep in the sling, and a good skunk caretaker would never startle his kit like that. So instead he said, "Thank you, Mom. And thank you, Janie. Thank you both."

CHAPTER 26

How to Know Someone

When Saturday came, Bat woke up feeling nervous. What if Israel wanted to hold Thor? Would Bat have to let him? What if Israel didn't like the snacks Bat and Mom had decided on—lemonade and crackers and apple slices and cheese?

Mom had asked Bat what kinds of food Israel liked and what he liked to do for fun, but Bat didn't have any answers. He hadn't ever noticed things like that.

"Most kids like to play handball at recess," he told her.

"Well, does Israel?"

Bat didn't know, but Mom said that was okay because they didn't have a handball, anyway.

"Maybe you boys could plant some of the seedlings," she suggested. Mom had little plastic pots of herbs growing in the sunny kitchen window, and now that it was getting warm, it was time to put them in the garden in the backyard.

"I don't know if Israel likes to plant things," Bat said.

"Most kids like to dig in the dirt," Mom said.

So when Israel and his dad arrived at eleven thirty, the first thing that Bat said when he answered the door was, "Do you like to garden?"

Israel shrugged. "I guess," he said.

"Bat," said Mom behind him, "invite them inside."

He was blocking the doorway, Bat realized. He stepped back and said, "Come in."

"Thanks," said Israel.

His dad said, "Thanks so much for inviting Israel over."

"Thanks for bringing him," said Mom. "I'm Valerie."

"Tom," said Israel's dad. They shook hands. Then he said, "I'm just going to run a few errands. Can I pick him up at two o'clock?"

After Israel's dad left, Bat said, "We have apples and cheese and crackers and lemonade. And Mom says we can plant the seedlings in the garden. And I guess if you want you can see my room."

"Actually," said Israel, "I was hoping to meet the skunk."

"Oh," said Bat. "Okay."

Thor was in his enclosure. He was getting big enough to walk now, but he still wasn't steady on his feet. He seemed to know that when Bat opened the enclosure door, it was something to be excited about, because he woke up and started scooting around.

"He's tiny!" Israel said.

Bat scooped up Thor and held him close. Thor could see now, but not very well. Skunks didn't have very good eyesight. "He's way bigger than he was," Bat said. "And he's got fur. When he was first born he was almost bald and he couldn't open his eyes or walk or anything."

"Can I hold him?" Israel asked, putting out his hands.

That sounded like a terrible idea to Bat. "Have you ever held a baby skunk before?"

"No," said Israel.

"I don't know," said Bat. "You might drop him."

"I could sit on the floor," Israel said, "and you could hand him to me."

Bat wanted to say no. But Mom said, "Bat, honey, you'd never held a skunk kit, either, before a few weeks ago. But you've never dropped Thor."

"I don't know," Bat said again. "Would you promise to be careful?"

"Yes," said Israel. "I promise."

Bat wanted to be sure that Israel was taking this seriously. That he understood how important this was, being careful with Thor. So he looked straight into Israel's eyes. Maybe he could see something in there, like Mom said. Something that would let him know it would be okay to trust Israel.

Israel's eyes were light green. They were framed by thick black eyelashes. Their pupils were round and black, just like everybody's pupils.

Bat wanted to see something in Israel's eyes. But all he saw were eyes.

Then he looked at Israel's hands, the way they were cupped together to form a safe little nest. He saw how Israel had overlapped his palms so that there was no way Thor could slip between them.

Bat didn't know much about eyes. But he knew about hands. Mom's hands, so strong and sure

when handling animals. Laurence's hands, enormous but gentle anyway. Mr. Grayson's hands, with long fingers and interesting rings. Dad's hands, with nails clipped short and neat. Janie's hands, so clever at braiding.

Israel's hands told Bat that Thor would be safe. So Bat placed the kit into them. He didn't even make Israel sit on the floor.

"Oh, he's so light!" Israel said. "He's so cute!"

"He's perfect," Bat said. "I'm going to learn everything there is to know about caring for skunks. Mom says we can keep Thor until he's old enough to release, and I'm going to become the best skunk caretaker in the world."

Israel brought Thor up close to his face and rubbed him against his cheek. "Do you think maybe you could teach me some stuff, too?" he asked.

"You want to learn about the care and feeding of skunks?" Bat asked.

"Yes," said Israel.

Maybe they could plant the seedlings the next time Israel came over. Maybe today they could talk about skunks, and research skunks, and watch YouTube videos about skunks.

"Okay," said Bat.

Israel handed Thor back to Bat, and Bat put on the sling and tucked Thor inside. He felt the skunk scratch and turn and then settle down to sleep.

"Well," Bat said, "do you want to see my room?"

"Sure," said Israel.

So Bat led the way through their little house, down the hall, and into his room. He opened the door. "After you," he said to Israel.

Before he followed Israel into the room, Bat turned to see Mom standing by the skunk enclosure. She was smiling, and she lifted her hand in a little wave. She looked happy. And Bat *felt* happy—really, really happy. He had a warm,

sleepy skunk kit in a pouch around his neck, and he had a boy—maybe even a friend—visiting his room, waiting to research skunks with him. Bat didn't know how things would turn out with Thor, and he didn't know how things would turn out with Israel, either. But right now, Bat felt as happy as he'd ever felt in his life. He waved back to his mom and felt his face stretch into a smile just as wide as hers.

And then, with Thor tucked safely into his pouch, Bat went into his room to hang out with his friend.

Author's Note

Believe it or not, there is a real Dr. Jerry Dragoo, and he really does run the Dragoo Institute for the Betterment of Skunks and Skunk Reputations!

Though the fictionalized Dr. Jerry Dragoo in this book responded to Bat with a rather short email message, the real Dr. Jerry Dragoo has written extensively about skunks—their origin, history, environment, diseases, and more. If a real-life child were to write to Dr. Jerry Dragoo about the pros and cons of skunk adoption, his answer would be much more complete than the fictional email included in *A Boy Called Bat*. As Dr. Jerry Dragoo would tell you, owning a skunk is a complicated matter, not to be taken lightly, and illegal in many places. Please visit his website at www.dragoo.org if you would like to learn more!

Heartfelt thanks to Dr. Jerry Dragoo for his input and advice.

Acknowledgments

The credit for the idea for *A Boy Called Bat* lies with Adah Nuchi, who reminded me that I like to write about little moments and unusual animals. Thank you, Adah, for seeing the heart of who I am as a writer.

The enthusiasm of Rubin Pfeffer for this project heartened me throughout the process, and I am so grateful for Jordan Brown, who loves Bat as much as I do and gently helped me make this book its very best self.

A special acknowledgment is due to my nephew Joseph Trogdor Kuczynski, who named Thor.

As always, thanks to my family of readers and my own little family at home, human and animal alike. I love you.